LION OF THE LAVABEDS

Walker A. Tompkins

CHIVERS
THORNDIKE

This Large Print book is published by BBC Audiobooks Ltd, Bath, England and by Thorndike Press®, Waterville, Maine, USA.

Published in 2005 in the U.K. by arrangement with Golden West Literary Agency

Published in 2005 in the U.S. by arrangement with Golden West Literary Agency

U.K. Hardcover   ISBN 1–4056–3287–9 (Chivers Large Print)
U.K. Softcover   ISBN 1–4056–3288–7 (Camden Large Print)
U.S. Softcover   ISBN 0–7862–7437–9 (Nightingale)

The text of this Large Print edition is unabridged.
Other aspects of the book may vary from the original edition.

Set in 16 pt. New Times Roman.

Printed in Great Britain on acid-free paper.

British Library Cataloguing in Publication Data available

Library of Congress Cataloging-in-Publication Data

Tompkins, Walker A.
　　Lion of the lavabeds / by Walker A. Tompkins.
　　　　p.　　cm.
　　ISBN 0–7862–7437–9 (lg. print : sc : alk. paper)
　　1. Indians of North America—Wars—Fiction. 2. Illegal arms transfers—Fiction. 3. Large type books. I. Title. II. Series.
PS3539.O3897L56 2005
813'.54—dc22
　　　　　　　　　　　　　　　　　　　　　　　　　2004030076

LION OF THE LAVABEDS

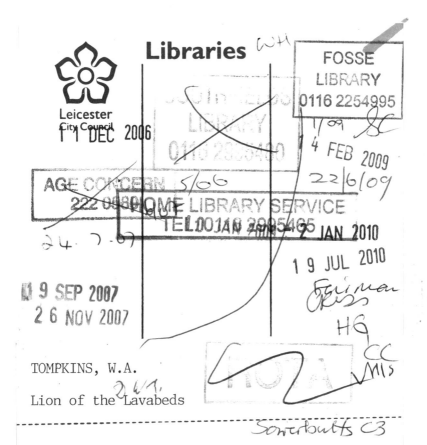

TOMPKINS, W.A.
Lion of the Lavabeds

CHAPTER ONE

MODOC MASSACRE

It was a small band of Indians, no larger than a scouting party, and it moved furtively through the undergrowth above the greening acres of Blake's Farm on ponies whose hoofs were encased in buckskin pouches to deaden the sound of their passage.

Daubs of ochre and iron oxide on their cheekbones and unwhiskered jaws branded them as renegade Modocs, though the traditional hunting ground of their tribe was in Klamath Lake Basin, north of the staggered skyline of the Siskiyou Range.

Only Kintupash, their chieftain, wore the habiliments of his ancestral Modocs. They were a fringed jacket of parfleche leather, with an elkhide baldric slanting from shoulder to thigh and sagging under the weight of an iron tomahawk, a sheathed scalping blade, and a rusty cap-and-ball pistol with a clover-leaf cylinder which had once been the property of a wagonmaster bound for California's gold fields with a Conestoga caravan.

Rawhide pants, thonged leggings and ankle-high moccasins completed Kintupash's costume. A long eagle feather jutted from his unkempt, short-bobbed hair as an insigne of

1

rank.

The other warriors in his scouting party were as ragtag as the motley cavalcade of stolen ponies they forked, wearing as they did the shirts and pants and scuffed boots of hapless Oregonian pioneers whose scalps now adorned their tomahawk handles. Unlike their dramatic, warbonneted cousins in remoter parts of the continent, such as the Sioux or the Mohawks or the Shawnee, these Modocs were a disheveled, dirty, flearidden band.

On the crest of a rise where the timber thinned, Kintupash lifted an arm in signal for his warriors to dismount and slither through the knee-high grass to a vantage point which gave them a view of the settler's cabin in the clearing below.

It was a pastoral scene, deceptively beautiful, giving no hint of the bloodthirsty, predatory men lurking at its borders. Far to the south the westering sun rays touched the brooding twin peaks of Shasta with rose and lavender, glistening off lesser snow fields of the Siskiyous.

*   *   *

Unbroken forest land stretched to horizons so remote they tired the eye and thrilled the spirit of the most jaded hunter. Only the log cabin and the brush corral down in the meadow hinted that this was the spring of '73 and that

2

white man had discovered this evergreen paradise hundreds of miles north of the California gold fields.

'She visits the paleface who built yonder cabin, Kintupash,' spoke the petty chieftain whose name was known to the bloody history of Oregon as Schonchin. 'Winema, daughter of your father's brother, who sleeps in the teepee of the hairy-faced one who speaks our tongue.'

Kintupash's obsidian-black eyes glittered with a hatred which had been responsible for the reign of terror now raging throughout southern Oregon. To the hated whites, Kintupash was known as 'Captain Jack' and an indictment for his capture had been issued by a civil court in Oregon, charging him with inciting the Modoc War which had run its bloody course through the winter just passed. Kintupash, who had carved himself a niche in frontier history as the 'Lion of the Lavabeds,' that impenetrable *pedregal* sprawled below the California border where Captain Jack and his Modoc tribesmen had taken refuge.

Captain Jack's beady gaze moved in keen appraisal of the stockaded cabin at the foot of the slope. Smoke curled lazily from a mud-and-wattle chimney. Two children, mere toddlers not long out of swaddling clothes, played inside the stockade, visible through the open gates. A farmer was plowing along a meandering creek.

Somewhere inside that cabin, consorting

3

with the sodbuster who had founded his little homestead here in the Siskiyou uplands, would be Winema, the squaw who served as an interpreter for the blue-coated soldiery at Fort Klamath. As such, Captain Jack considered Winema to be a traitor to her race, a squaw whose scalp would soon adorn his trophy-hung baldric. It was doubly galling to the chief to have Schonchin remind him that Winema was his own blood cousin.

Vengeance had been the motive which had drawn Captain Jack out of the Lavabeds and drawn him to this isolated settlement in the tall timber. Blake's Ranch it was called, and of itself constituted no great prize for Captain Jack's Modocs. A half-dozen scalps, a few horses, perhaps a few knives and guns—no more.

'We attack now,' Captain Jack grunted in the guttural undertones of his Modoc tongue. 'We burn the cabin and the haystack. Winema and the paleface she calls husband must die by my hand. It is understood?'

The Modocs nodded, gripping their scalping knives and their gun stocks with an impatience not long to be held in curb.

Like wraiths skulking through the tall grass, Captain Jack and his dozen-odd warriors moved back to where their ponies waited. A quick blow without warning, the flash of a torch and a swift thunder of gunshots, and they would be well on their way back to the

Lavabeds before nightfall. And the blood of the traitoress Winema would stain Captain Jack's hands as proof of his revenge . . .

Jed Blake was driving his plow horse up from the creek when the attack came. Without warning, the edge of the forest came alive with whooping red devils and his speared horse was spilling its entrails over the new furrows before the red-whiskered pioneer had time to unsling his musket.

Blake's shout of warning reached the camp where his wife Jennie was preparing a meal for their guests, Winema Riddle and her white husband, Frank. The shout was cut off by an arrow which winged its way from a war bow to imbed itself in the sodbuster's throat.

It was Frank Riddle, the Fort Klamath interpreter, who sprinted across the stockade to swing shut and bolt the big gates, even as the Modoc massacre party swarmed across the clearing behind smoke-gouting rifles. There were eight souls in the beleaguered cabin, only three adults among them. Frank Riddle was the only man.

By the time Riddle had gathered the Blake children safely inside the log farmhouse, the sod roof was blazing where Modoc arrows, dipped in bear grease and rolled with gunpowder before being ignited with flint and steel, had sped like fiery comets over the pointed logs of the protecting stockade.

Within ten minutes at the most, the pole rafters would cave in over the heads of those in the cabin, facing them with the dilemma of being burned alive or being forced out into the open to be cut down by the marauding Modocs who were now circling the stockade on their fleet ponies.

'We are doomed, Mrs. Blake,' Riddle said gravely, as he stood beside the Modoc woman who was his wife. 'No one could know that the Modocs would venture this far from the Lavabeds, knowing that the Army has surrounded their hideout.'

Tears misted the pioneer woman's eyes as she tried to quiet her sobbing children. With her husband scalped and mutilated out at the edge of the clearing, death no longer held any terrors for Blake's widow.

'Wait!' cried Winema, from her station by one of the rifle ports in the log walls. 'Captain Jack is withdrawing! Something is scaring the Indians away!'

Riddle and Mrs. Blake rushed to the loophole. Winema's words were true. The whooping Modoc braves, instead of closing in for the kill, were galloping toward the hemming forest in panicky retreat.

Then, to the ears of the stunned prisoners under the burning room, came a dull rumble of many hoofbeats. Out of the clearing to the south, from the direction of the trail leading to Mount Shasta and the southern settlements, rode two horsemen firing at the retreating Indians and spurring toward the stockaded enclosure.

Frank Riddle was at the gate sliding back the bars when he saw that one of the riders wore the blue uniform with yellow outseamed pants legs indicating the U.S. Cavalry. His companion was a handsome, swarthy-faced young Mexican wearing the high-peaked sombrero and bannering rainbow-hued serape of a California *hidalgo* from Old Mexico.

'How many of you here?' demanded the blue-coated rider, on whose shoulders were the bars of an Army captain.

'Five children, two women and myself,' Riddle answered, cocking his head to catch the fading rumble of hoofs off beyond the clearing. 'You are bringing a detachment of cavalry?'

The young captain flung himself off his lather-flecked mouse-dun cavalry horse and shook his head.

'That was a bluff to scare off those redskins,' he said grimly. 'My friend Celestino Mireles here and myself stampeded a herd of hosses we found grazin' down the creek bottom in the hopes it would deceive them Modocs. I am Captain Bob Pryor, heading for Twenty-first Infantry headquarters on special duty.'

The women and children gathered around Riddle as the interpreter stared at Pryor, comprehension dawning slowly in his eyes.

'Then—you two are alone? The two of you scared off that massacre attack?'

Celestino Mireles' dusky face was grave as he nodded.

'Eet ees true, senor. And eef the *Indios* circle back, they weel find out the treek. We must get away from thees *casa* pronto or we weel lose our hair, *es verdad!*'

CHAPTER TWO

RIO KID'S MISSION

Time was precious. Pryor had gambled his own scalp on the off chance that the small party of Indians which he had caught in the act of attacking Blake's Farm would hear the stampeding herd of horses and, catching sight of his own cavalry uniform, reach the conclusion that Army reinforcements were providentially close at hand to outnumber the attackers.

Pryor's scheme had worked. The Modocs had withdrawn at the first glimpse of his uniform, no doubt believing that another troop of cavalry was coming up from Camp Bidwell to augment the Army laying siege to the

Lavabeds. Celestino Mireles, in his Mexican costume, had probably been mistaken for a California scout leading the soldiers northward.

But if the Modocs sent a scout back to reconnoiter, Bob Pryor knew his coup might easily be turned into a disaster. There was not even time enough for Mrs. Blake to rush back into the blazing cabin and recover a few precious personal belongings.

Riddle and his Indian wife had their saddle horses inside the stockade. The Blakes' stock, on the other hand, were among the animals pasturing down on the creek, which Pryor and Mireles had stampeded.

With feverish haste, Pryor ordered the children mounted, together with their mother, on the four available horses. Then, the saddlers carrying double, the fugitives galloped away from the blazing cabin and vanished into the forest bordering the creek which bisected the clearing.

Out of view of Modoc scouts, Pryor and Celestino shook out lariats and headed downstream, returning shortly with two ponies each from Blake's scattered remuda. The pioneer's children, even the toddlers, were at home on horseback.

'The nearest refuge is the sawmill camp, owned by Miles Elkorn, Captain,' Frank Riddle reported. 'We will be safe from Captain Jack there. We can reach Elkorn's by moonrise.'

They headed north, traveling by game trails which Winema, the squaw, as leader of the cavalcade picked out. The children's horses were spaced between the adult riders, with Captain Bob Pryor bringing up the rear. They rode without speech, pushing their horses with the utmost caution over the pine-needle carpet of the trail, realizing that Captain Jack and his raiding party might well be lurking in ambuscade at any bend of the trail.

The imposed silence of their getaway flight prevented Riddle or the Blake family from asking the questions which tormented them regarding the identity of their rescuers.

Elsewhere in the West, Captain Robert Pryor was better known as the 'Rio Kid.' He was a husky, handsome man in the prime of life, riding the saddle with military erectness which dated back to his Army service in the Civil War.

Born and bred on the banks of the Rio Grande, Pryor had volunteered for duty with the Union Army at the outbreak of the great conflict between the States, becoming chief scout for such noted generals as Sheridan and Custer, Meade and Sherman.

After the victory at Appomattox, the Rio Kid had returned to his parents' ranch in Texas. There he had found that tragedy had visited his stamping grounds during his absence, Border bandits having wiped out his family and ruined the home spread. This crushing blow had altered the course of Pryor's life, and had been the motivating force back of his pledge to wage relentless war against lawlessness in all its forms.

Celestino Mireles, his Mexican *compadre*, had a similar background of family tragedy. He had been Pryor's inseparable companion since the long-past day when the Rio Kid had rescued the Mexican youth from Border renegades who had slain his father and mother in their *hacienda*.

No mere coincidence of destiny had brought the Rio Kid and Celestino Mireles into this isolated pocket of California's rugged Siskiyous today, in time to thwart Captain Jack's vicious attempt to massacre his cousin, Winema. They rode on Army orders.

*   *   *

The Modoc War had been raging on the Oregon-California border since the previous autumn, the outgrowth of the Modocs' vow to wipe out the white settlers of southern Oregon.

From what little the Rio Kid had learned of the campaign, things had been going badly for the Army during the past winter and spring. Led by their crafty chieftain, Captain Jack, the Modocs had consolidated their forces and withdrawn into the vast *pedregal* region below

11

Tule Lake known as the Lavabeds.

There, standing off superior odds, the Modocs had defied every assault of American cavalry, infantry, and artillery units. As a result, no less a personage than President Ulysses S. Grant, Commander-in-Chief of the Army, had dispatched Captain Robert Pryor to the West with orders to assist in breaking the deadlock between the Modocs and the attacking military forces.

According to the orders in the Rio Kid's tunic, he was to report on arrival in Northern California at the outpost run by the American sawyer, Miles Elkorn. For that reason, the Kid was doubly anxious to reach the end of tonight's getaway trail.

Strangely enough, the Rio Kid had heard of his trail guide, Winema, by reputation. The Modoc woman's fame had spread far abroad through the land. Pryor had heard her name mentioned frequently in Monterey and San Francisco within the past fortnight.

Daughter of a Modoc medicine man, wife of the white interpreter who had greeted Pryor at the entrance of Blake's stockade, Winema was already fast becoming a legend, known for her exploits in behalf of the white settlers as the 'Oregon Pocahontas.'

It struck Pryor as an odd vagary of Fate that his introduction to the Modoc War should have been through Winema herself.

As they rode through the gathering

12

darkness of the fir timberland, the Rio Kid peered along the file of jogging horses to study Winema. He saw that she was as beautiful as her name, a charming specimen of Indian womanhood at its finest.

Clad in beaded doeskin blouse and skirt, Winema rode her leggy blue roan pony without benefit of saddle, her youthful body swaying to the mount's gait with the lithe ease of a born rider. Her raven-black hair hung in twin braids down her back, combed back off a copper-complexioned face that was molded in the same clean-cut lines which characterized Indians of the Great Plains, and rarely found among the decadent coastal tribes.

Her husband, Frank Riddle, was a powerfully built man in his early forties. Strength of character was evident in his distinguished features and dignified bearing which automatically discounted the stigma usually attached to an inter-racial marriage.

Even without knowing Riddle's contribution to the Modoc War, the Rio Kid knew Winema's husband did not merit the slur denoted by the popular term 'squawman.' Riddle had wed a thoroughbred, whatever the color of her skin or the savagery of her ancestors.

Night fell ebon black over the Siskiyous. The procession of horses moved in a compact formation along the tenuous forest trails. A sickle of lemon-yellow moon was cruising over

13

the lofty broken crown of Mount Shasta, remote in the indigo distance, when they emerged on a logged-off mountain valley to see the lights of Miles Elkorn's sawmill camp twinkling in the distance.

Sentries hailed them from the blockhouse bastions built on the four corners of Elkorn's stockade, as the file of riders drew closer, threading through the stump-dotted flats in the moonlight.

'Winema, northbound from Blake's Farm!' the Modoc girl answered the challenge as they reined up before the closed gates of Elkorn's lumber camp. 'Captain Jack attacked the farm this afternoon and killed Mr. Blake in cold blood! We seek shelter.'

The big gates swung open to admit the riders to the sawmill compound. They were quickly surrounded by a swarm of buckskin-clad trappers, mountain men and loggers. Mrs. Blake and her little family were well-known here and the news of the homesteader's brutal killing came as a stunning shock to the whiskered frontiersmen who gathered to welcome the survivors.

*   *   *

After their horses had been turned over to one of Elkorn's hostlers, the Rio Kid and Celestino Mireles were approached by a towering giant of a man who wore a blanket-lined mackinaw, raccoon cap and high-laced mountaineer boots.

'I'm Miles Elkorn,' the big man said with bluff camaraderie, shaking Pryor's hand. 'Riddle tells me yuh're Captain Pryor?'

The Rio Kid nodded, appraising the famous California lumber king. Elkorn wore long cinnamon-red Dundreary whiskers which partially offset the smallpox scars which disfigured his otherwise aristocratic face. Elkorn's deep-set eyes were overshadowed by craggy brows threaded with premature gray.

'That's right,' Pryor acknowledged, and introduced Celestino. 'My orders from President Grant were to report to you, Elkorn. I understand yuh're to conduct me to the commanding officer in charge of the Modoc campaign.'

Elkorn's granite-gray eyes were somber.

'Things ain't goin' well, Captain,' he said. 'Captain Jack is lickin' the pants off the whole U.S. Army, to date. We need a man of yore caliber here. But come inside. Some roast venison and California pheasant should be welcome under yore belt, eh?'

After a night's sleep, Pryor and Celestino, accompanied by Elkorn, breakfasted in the black hour before dawn. They had reached the marshy rim of Tule Lake, three miles from the sawmill, by the time sunrise flung its gaudy banners over the Lavabeds. Their host, Miles Elkorn, had insisted on getting an early start for the reason that the commanding officer of the armies assembled in Northern California was rarely at his headquarters after ten o'clock in the morning.

Tule Lake's blue-gray waters were like crinkled parchment under the light breeze which swept off the snow-covered Siskiyous. Across the wildfowl-dotted lake, the Rio Kid could see the frowning *pedregal* of the Lavabeds sloping down to meet the water, where mountains of molten rock had congealed at the water's edge in millenniums past.

Even at a distance, Pryor realized the tough campaign which the Americans faced in attempting to rout the Modocs from their craggy lair. A high plateau, literally a frozen sea of petrified volcanic stone, the Lavabeds were perhaps the most inaccessible area of badlands in the entire West.

The sun was an hour high when Pryor and Mireles topped a rise and caught sight of the Stars and Stripes floating above a tent city in the distance.

'Field headquarters of Brevet Major Tracy Williard's Twenty-first U.S. Infantry,' Miles Elkorn explained. 'The staffs of attached complements are here—the California Volunteer Rifles, a few howitzer batteries from Camp Harney, Oregon, and the First Brigade of Oregon Mounted Militia.'

Pryor nodded thoughtfully. A powerful

16

concentration of troops had been massed here at the edge of the Lavabeds for months, only to chalk up defeat after defeat at the hands of Captain Jack and a band of warriors numbering not more than six hundred. Scanning the Lavabeds in the background, the Rio Kid saw where a million soldiers could easily be slaughtered in an effort to storm the Modocs' redoubt.

Twenty minutes later a blue-uniformed sentry challenged them, saluted as he caught sight of Pryor's bars, grinned a friendly greeting to Miles Elkorn, and admitted them to the headquarters parade ground.

They dismounted in front of a tent which, because of the flagstaff at its rear, they knew to be Major Williard's headquarters. Miles Elkorn approached an aide who emerged from the tent and after a moment's conversation, turned to the Rio Kid and Celestino.

'We're in luck, gentlemen,' the lumber king said. 'Major Williard has not yet ridden out to the battlefield. He'll see yuh, Captain Pryor.'

Removing his campaign hat with its crossed-sabers insignia of the U.S. Cavalry, the Rio Kid ducked through the fly of the tent and came stiffly to attention as he faced a tall, barrel-chested officer seated behind a table spread with battle maps.

'Captain Robert Pryor reportin' for special duty, sir,' the Rio Kid said. 'Here are my orders from President Grant.'

17

CHAPTER THREE

SUICIDE ASSIGNMENT

Brevet Major Tracy Williard's work-gaunted face was revitalized as he came around from behind the table and shook the Rio Kid's hand, then accepted the envelope from Washington, D.C.

'I have been expecting you, Captain,' Williard said. 'I have heard a great deal of your exploits in the past. It may surprise you to know that the entire outcome of this campaign may rest on your shoulders alone, sir.'

Pryor seated himself in a canvas-bottomed field chair as Williard went back and began shuffling papers behind his desk. Williard was a battle-scarred old veteran of Bull Run and Gettysburg whose bearded face reminded Pryor of General U. S. Grant himself.

'Assuming that you are not cognizant with the background of the Modoc campaign,' Williard began once more in his brusk military fashion, 'I shall risk boring you by bringing you up-to-date on developments. First, however— what is your attitude where Indian fighting is concerned, Captain Pryor?'

The Rio Kid hesitated. He was friendly toward the redmen and Indian campaigns were somewhat out of his line.

'Well,' he said tentatively, 'the Great White Father back in Washington hasn't a spotless record insofar as his treatment of the redman is concerned, Major. The Indians were here before the whites came, and in many cases they've been treated pretty shabby, what with broken treaties and the like. For a man who has dedicated his life to help downtrodden people and persecuted folks I ain't exactly what yuh'd call an Indian-hater.'

Major Williard flushed before Pryor's blunt frankness.

'Well spoken, son,' he grinned. 'However, you need feel no compunction about assisting in crushing these Modoc scalp-hunters. The Modocs are the scourge of the West, feared and hated by even their neighboring tribes—the Klamaths, the Umatillas, the Me-Yuks.'

The Rio Kid listened with respectful attention as Williard unfolded one of the bloodiest chapters in the history of the winning of the West.

History supported his assertion that since the earliest period of Oregon's settlement, the Modocs, or *maklaks* as they called themselves, had been noted for their warlike ways and the extreme cruelties which they inflicted on their captives.

In 1865, the Modoc and Klamath tribes had voluntarily ceded their lands to the United States, which were surveyed and thrown open to emigrants eager to leave the East, then in

19

the throes of the Reconstruction period following the Civil War. But the Modocs had broken their solemn treaty with the whites by bolting their reservation. At the instigation of Chief Kintupash, now popularly known as Captain Jack, the Modocs had gone on a red warpath which threatened the white settlers with extermination.

Seeing Oregon's future in peril, agents at the Camp Yainax reservation had appealed to the Army for help. The noted General E. R. S. Canby, in command of the Columbia Department, had arrived on the scene with his troops. In their opening engagement with Captain Jack's band, General Canby had been defeated with heavy losses, but had forced Captain Jack and his allied bands to withdraw into the fastnesses of the California Lavabeds.

'A month or so ago, on April eleventh,' Major Williard explained, 'a Peace Commission was formed with General Canby at its head. They met Captain Jack and his sub-chiefs in a pow-wow, hoping to smoke the peace pipe. During the council, Captain Jack drew a pistol and shot General Canby in the back. All of the Commission would have lost their lives had it not been for the quick work of Winema, the Modoc squaw who was acting as an interpreter.'

The Rio Kid nodded.

'I have met Winema and Frank Riddle,' he said. 'She says that Captain Jack regards her as a traitor to her tribe.'

'Perhaps, from his viewpoint,' Williard agreed. 'Personally, I believe Winema is working for the good of her people. The tribe is mesmerized by Captain Jack's malevolent personality. This is a big land, Winema feels, with ample room for whites and reds to live together peaceably. Winema is a fine woman. She is loved and respected by the majority of the Modocs.'

*   *   *

Major Williard shuffled through his maps and papers. He appeared like a man aged and broken before his time.

'It is nearly June,' he said, 'and frankly, Captain Pryor, the situation is deadlocked. The most we can say is that we have the Modoc tribe surrounded in the Lavabeds, making it impossible for them to get out.'

The Rio Kid kept his thoughts to himself. Remembering Captain Jack's abortive raid of yesterday, he had reason to doubt that the Modocs were as bottled up as Major Williard would have him believe.

'The Modocs could live in the Lavabeds indefinitely,' Williard said. 'Winema tells me they have an artesian well—they call it the "Fountain of the Gods"—which gives them an inexaustible supply of water. Now Washington is howling for action. I expect momentarily to

21

be relieved of my command.

'Our troops' morale is high. They want to avenge General Canby's brutal murder. Volunteers from both Oregon and California are fighting with the regular Army. But we are getting nowhere.'

The Rio Kid leaned forward to study the sketchy maps of the Lavabeds. It was a wild, rugged land, as he already knew, forty-five hundred feet above sea level, crisscrossed with deep canyons and honeycombed with innumerable caves and subterranean river beds. The Modocs could move at will through the Lavabeds, secure even against the shell-fire of American artillery.

'Sir, how about starvin 'em out?' he suggested.

Williard grinned bleakly. 'That, Pryor, is the crux of the whole problem. Captain Jack is getting help from unknown sources. Quartermaster supply wagons have been robbed—we believe by white renegades—and the rifles, blankets, food and other supplies those wagons contained are being smuggled through our siege lines.'

'Then these white renegades must be caught!'

'Precisely. Until Captain Jack's source of supplies is cut off and the traitors who are helping him prolong this useless war are brought to justice, we can't hope to bring the Modoc campaign to a conclusion. I don't mind admitting that I am at the end of my wits, Captain Pryor.'

'Where,' asked the Rio Kid, 'do I come in, Major?'

Williard unlocked a field safe and drew out an envelope with the red borders which designated it as being Top Secret.

He handed the missive to the young Texan with an expression which defined better than words his very great reluctance at having to give the Rio Kid his official orders.

'Your mission sounds simple enough,' the Gettysburg veteran said, 'but I feel it only fair to warn you that President Grant has dispatched you out here on—on a suicide assignment. You will read these orders, memorize them, and then I shall destroy them.'

The Rio Kid felt his pulses quicken as he read:

SUBJECT: Reconnaissance mission
             to Lavabeds.
FROM: Commanding General, Dept.
             of Columbia.
TO: Captain Robert Pryor, Cavalry
             Corps.

1. You are hereby instructed to penetrate the Lavabeds and report to this command the exact location of Captain Jack's supply depots and the number of warriors, including noncombatants and casualties, which he

commands.

2. You are to conduct personal intelligence investigation into identity of renegades believed to be smuggling ammunition and food supplies to Modocs.

The orders were signed on behalf of the now-dead General E. R. S. Canby, commander of the Columbia Department, by his adjutant, Captain Tracy Williard, who had since been given an honorary brevet commission to give him adequate command of field operations in the Lavabeds campaign.

'Am I to have a free hand in carryin' out this assignment?' the Rio Kid inquired, handing the orders back to his superior. Williard nodded. 'Good! First, then, I aim to investigate folks in this territory who have the means to carry supplies to Captain Jack, sir. That would probably be a trader who can get hold of wagons, wheelwrights, and hay and grain for his teams.'

Pryor leaned over the table, studying a map of the region.

'In other words,' he explained, 'I want to know where the nearest town is, where I might find a man who would stand to make a profit sellin' supplies to the Modocs.'

Major Williard tapped a finger on one of his maps.

'That's easy. Stateline, here, is the only settlement in this area. It's a way point on the

24

wagon route between Yreka and the Rogue River Valley settlements.'

* * *

Consulting the chart, Pryor saw that Stateline was situated on a bend of Lost River.

It straddled the Oregon-California line and was roughly fifteen miles from Williard's camp.

'I'll start out,' the Rio Kid decided, 'by payin' a visit to this here Stateline and scoutin' the tradin' posts there. One other thing before I go, Major. Is Miles Elkorn to be trusted?'

Williard nodded emphatically.

'Absolutely. Not only is Elkorn the wealthiest settler in Northern California, but he has timber holdings and mining claims which give him a motive for wanting to see the Modocs exterminated. Miles Elkorn has been of incalculable value to our campaign to date. That is why General Grant's orders read for you to get in touch with Elkorn upon your arrival here.'

The Rio Kid came to attention, saluted, right-about-faced and headed for the flap of the tent.

'Yuh'll see me next,' he promised, 'after I've badgered the Lion of the Lavabeds in his den. Good day, Major Williard.'

Williard passed a hand over his eyes as he saw the canvas tent fly fall back to cover the

Rio Kid's exit. The old campaigner would have wagered his chances of promotion, in that moment, on the probability of never seeing the Rio Kid alive again . . .

*   *   *

Sundown hues were burning out in the west when Robert Pryor finished his journey northward from Miles Elkhorn's lumber camp and reined up his cavalry horse, Saber, on a bluff overlooking Lost River and the isolated settlement of Stateline.

He bore little resemblance to the sprucely uniformed cavalry officer who had arrived at Miles Elkorn's sawmill camp the night before. Upon their return from Williard's camp, Elkorn had outfitted him in a buckskin jacket, a miner's shirt of red flannel, corduroy pants, and shabby, run-down mountain boots.

Buckled over the buckskin blouse were his Colt .45 six-guns, the only accoutrement of his former attire which the Rio Kid had retained. To the casual eye, he resembled any one of a thousand mountaineers or prospectors in the region. Topping off the garb was a coontail cap.

Celestino Mireles, on the other hand, had retained his Old Mexican costume—braided gaucho jacket, flare-bottomed *charro* pants with silver tie-conchas bordering the red velvet triangle sewed along the outseams, fancy

Chihuahuan spurs with star rowels, and the red sash, bright serape and ball-tasseled sombrero of his native land.

They were accompanied on their ride up from Elkorn's place by Frank Riddle and Winema and a young handlebar-mustached enlisted man from Major Williard's 21st Infantry, Sergeant Walker Henry.

The sergeant was riding to Stateline to pick up a squad of recruits from the Rogue River country.

'There you have it, Captain,' Sergeant Henry explained, gesturing with an arm toward the sprawl of false-fronted saloons, log-walled hurdygurdy houses, corrals and soddies which made up the river town. 'Stateline, wildest hell-hole this side of the Mother Lode gold camps. You shouldn't have far to look for villains in that uncurried neck of purgatory, I guarantee you that.'

Pryor tossed the bushy coontail back over his shoulder and stared moodily at the smoking chimneys of Stateline, watching the outlines of the main street grow dim as the light waned.

Traffic teemed on that crooked street which followed the bend of Lost River. Muleskinners drove pack trains across the shallow river ford, northbound for the Oregon settlements with peltries for the Portland market. Canvas-hooded freight wagons were parked in endless rows along the river front, lifeblood of the arteries of commerce which webbed out from Stateline to all points of the compass.

'We'll split up here and ride into town separately, folks,' the Rio Kid said, hipping over in his saddle to regard his trail mates. 'It won't hurt for you, Sergeant, to be seen ridin' into Stateline with Riddle and Winema here, since it's known they are employed by the Army.'

Sergeant Henry nodded and grinned.

'I understand, sir,' he said, 'your desire to pose as a mere trapper or hunter, with no Army connections. I shan't recognize you if I pass you on the street.'

Pryor turned to his Mexican *compadre.*

'For the time bein', Celestino, it'll be just as well if Stateline don't know you and I are together. Yuh may be asked questions. If so, pose as a *hidalgo* from some big *hacienda* down around Los Angeles.'

Celestino Mireles' white teeth flashed in a smile.

'*Si*, General,' the Mexican answered, using the nickname he habitually reserved for his partner of the out-trails. 'I weel be waiting at the Cascades Leevery Barn wheech Senora Winema told us about.'

CHAPTER FOUR

GUN BOSS OF STATELINE

Sergeant Henry touched his horse's flanks with steel and vanished down the tree-lined trail. Winema reined her blue roan closer alongside Pryor's dun, and her low, modulated voice held a note of worry as she spoke to him.

'The loggers at Elkorn's mill know you are the famous Rio Kid,' the Modoc girl reminded him. 'They come to Stateline to drink their firewater and dance with the bad women. They cannot be trusted to keep your secret.'

The Rio Kid smiled down at the Indian girl.

'That's so, Winema. But you and yore husband are the only folks I've told my plans to, knowin' yuh may be in a position to help me. The lumberjacks at Elkorn's place may not see anything out of the way in my change of clothes.'

She nodded, and dropped back.

Celestino Mireles was the next to break away from the group, riding down through the gathering darkness to await his partner at the livery stable which Winema had recommended.

'You are trying to find out who might be selling supplies to the Modocs,' Frank Riddle commented. 'I am going to give you a bit of

29

information for what it may be worth. In Stateline, the rougher element acknowledges no law except that of gun and knife. And the gun boss of Stateline is a trader who runs a wagon freight line between Yreka and Jacksonville.'

The Rio Kid's brows arched quizzically.

'His name?' he inquired softly.

'Dorian Fiske,' Riddle answered. 'A bad man, a killer. You will probably find him this evening at his saloon, the Golden Poppy Bar. Or perhaps at his freight barns, which he calls the Bon Marche Warehouse. It is there he stores his trade goods.'

The Rio Kid gathered up his reins and urged Saber down onto the trail.

'Thanks, Riddle,' he called back. 'Remember, I'm a fur trapper from the redwoods country, if anybody should ask. And if yuh meet me on the street, yuh don't know me from Adam. *Adios, amigos.*'

In minutes Pryor was sending his mouse-colored dun splashing along the muddy street of Stateline, keeping well against the crowded boardwalks to avoid the heavy-wheeled wagons which jammed the street. He passed up a dozen-odd saloons and gambling halls before he caught sight of a towering barn, constructed of whipsawed lumber from Elkorn's mill, whose false front advertised it to be the Bon Marche Trade Goods Warehouse.

Dorian Fiske's barn was locked and

deserted-looking. The Rio Kid continued on down the street, drawn to a rambling log-walled structure with whale-oil flares guttering at the eaves of its wooden-awninged porch. As he drew into the dancing firelight, he saw that the flares illuminated a gaudy sign. Gilt letters informed him that this was the:

GOLDEN POPPY SALOON
Dorian Fiske, Prop.

'Fiske's quite the hi-you-mucky-muck of Stateline, if he runs the town's biggest whisky den,' the Rio Kid muttered, finding a spot for Saber at the crowded hitch-rack. 'The kind of feller who might well be willin' to sell out his countrymen for the stolen gold Captain Jack's Modocs would pay him for contraband supplies.'

Shouldering through the batwings of the Golden Poppy, the Rio Kid was amazed at the elegance of this frontier saloon. Imported crystal chandeliers illuminated the crowded barroom: ornate mirrors, polished to vivid brilliance, adorned the backbar; in place of rough-hewn puncheons, the floor was covered with hardwood in elaborate parquet designs.

*   *   *

A gambling hall off to the left of the bar was crowded with miners, mule skinners, lumberjacks and freighters, staking their gold at the faro bank and roulette layout, the chuck-a-luck cage and the numerous poker tables. To the right was a dancehall where roughly-dressed mountain men whirled silken-gowned percentage girls on a polished maple floor to music supplied by a tin-panny orchestra of banjos, fiddles and a rickety piano.

In an effort to make himself inconspicuous, the Rio Kid found himself a spot at the bar and ordered brandy. The bartender had hardly placed bottle and glass before him than Pryor felt a jovial hand slap him on the back.

'The Rio Kid, in person!' boomed a friendly voice. 'I come from the Texas Panhandle myself, son. Heard plenty about yuh when I was punchin' longhorns after the war.'

Pryor groaned as he turned to see a lumberjack who had shared his bunkhouse at Elkorn's camp the night before. He could not recall the logger's name, but the Texan had spoken so loudly that the Rio Kid found himself the focal point of curious stares on all sides.

'From Texas, eh?' he said boredly, signaling the barkeep for another glass. 'Have some *aguardiente* with me?'

While they were watching the amber glow of the liquor, the logger kept up a running flow of conversation, mainly about his bad luck in the Mother Lode gold camps and his eventual

32

arrival at Miles Elkorn's sawmill in Northern California.

'Been here two winters, eh?' the Rio Kid remarked. 'Yuh ought to know the owner of this place, then. Dorian Fiske. Could yuh point him out to me?'

The logger, already in his cups, swung his bleary gaze over the smoke-clouded room, then gestured vaguely toward the door leading to the dancehall.

'That'sh Dorian Fishke yander, Rio Kid!' the lumberjack announced. 'Jush' stand here a shecond, Kid, an' I'll fotch him over here an' interdooce him to yuh. Fishke is the curly wolf of this burg. Fashtest gun draw in Californy, bar none.'

Before Pryor could protest, the logger was lurching down the bar toward a tall, frock-coated man who was standing by the dancehall entrance, aloof from the crowd.

Dropping a gold octagonal on the mahogany to pay for his brandy, the Rio Kid headed unobtrusively for the batwings. He didn't like the way things were shaping up. His casual question to Elkorn's logger had backfired. He had no desire for Dorian Fiske to have him pointed as the Rio Kid, an Army officer now masquerading in buckskins.

Slipping out into the night, the Rio Kid walked up to a window and peered inside. His drunken logger friend had sprawled flat on the floor and two housemen were dragging him toward a back entrance. He would sober up in the muddy gutter outside.

Grinning with relief, the Rio Kid swung his gaze toward Dorian Fiske, grateful for a chance to size up the gunboss of Stateline. Frank Riddle believed Fiske would bear watching as a potential renegade smuggler working in collusion with the beleaguered Lion of the Lavabeds, Captain Jack.

Fiske appeared to be in his late thirties, his high cheekbones and coarse black hair hinting of a strain of Indian blood in his own veins. He wore the white buckwing collar and string tie of a gambler. Six-guns were buckled at his thighs, the holsters snugged down against his ribbed marseilles pants.

Even at a distance, Pryor could sense the utter ruthlessness of the man whose guns ruled this bawdy trail town.

Leaving the Golden Poppy, the Rio Kid walked down an alley flanking the saloon, heading for a dingy hotel on a back street which he had spotted on his way into town. If rooms were available there, he would book one and return to see about Saber's grooming and graining for the night.

On the morrow, he would make a thorough reconnaissance of Stateline, checking on all trading posts in the town and conferring with Frank Riddle and Winema on the backgrounds of the traders who ran them. If this failed to uncover any leads, he planned to find

Celestino Mireles and make a scouting trip into the Lavabeds to carry out the first of Major Williard's secret orders.

*   *   *

He was emerging on the back street when the blow came, from behind. His only warning of danger was a scuffle of boots in the mud behind the saloon, and the whistle of a gun barrel zipping in a short arc toward his head.

Before the Rio Kid could duck and get a gun from leather, something exploded against his coonskin cap and his knees caved under him, plunging him into a black vortex in which he knew no pain, no sensations of any kind. It was complete oblivion . . .

Icy water splashing his face brought the Rio Kid back from the spinning void that had engulfed him. As consciousness returned it brought a stifling sense of confinement which he soon interpreted as a blindfold knotted over his eyes and ropes trussing his arms to his sides and binding his legs at knees and ankles.

Then a bottle neck was reamed between his teeth and he found himself gagging on forty-rod whisky. He swallowed a gulp of the fiery liquor, felt it sting his vitals and clear the dull, throbbing agony under his skull.

Then, as if from a remote distance, he heard a hoarse masculine voice calling him by name.

'Pryor! Robert Pryor! Yuh feel up to

35

answerin' a few questions, Captain?'

The Rio Kid shook his head dazedly. He still felt stupefied from the results of his pistol-whipping. All sense of time or space was lost to him. But his captor had addressed him by his military title of rank! His Captaincy was a secret.

'Yuh surprised that I know yuh're an Army spy, Rio Kid?' taunted the voice, above him. 'Yore secret wasn't kept well, Captain. Yuh come to Stateline straight from Major Williard's quarters. Yuh're workin' under secret orders. What are yore orders, Pryor?'

The Rio Kid struggled to a sitting position. Rough hands gripped his trussed arms and slid him around, pushing him back against what appeared to be a wall of unbarked logs.

'What are yore secret orders, Captain Pryor?' the voice demanded urgently. 'Who or what was yuh lookin' for in town tonight? Why did yuh go to the Golden Poppy?'

The Rio Kid clamped his mouth grimly. He had no idea who was speaking to him. The voice had familiar overtones, yet gave him no clue to its owner's identity. Where he was and how long he had been unconscious were riddles equally unanswerable.

'Take off this blindfold,' he panted. 'I want to see who I'm talkin' to.'

A grating laugh answered him.

'Yuh're a spy, Captain Pryor. In time of war—even the Modoc War—spies know the

36

price of failure. But yore life'll be spared if yuh tell me what you and Major Williard are plannin'.'

The Rio Kid shook his head slowly from side to side, the torture of his muddled brain striking nausea in the pit of his stomach. His nostrils detected the faint odor of human sweat and tobacco above the whisky fumes.

'An Army spy,' he retorted, 'wouldn't be worth the powder to blow him to Hades if he told anybody his orders.'

A weighty silence followed his defiance. Pryor heard shell belts creak as his captor changed position.

'Pryor,' he was asked, 'did yuh ever hear of Boston Charley and Hooker Jim?'

The Rio Kid nodded, remembering Major Williard's reference to Captain Jack's sub-chieftains that morning when the commanding officer of the 21st Infantry was outlining the progress of the Modoc campaign.

'Boston Charley and Hooker Jim are waitin' within earshot of this spot, Pryor,' his captor said grimly. 'They're Indians, of the most bloodthirsty breed. They'll have ways of makin' yuh tell yore secret which I, a civilized white man, wouldn't think of doin'. Want I should bring my Modoc friends here?'

Despair made the hairs on the Rio Kid's neck-nape lift but he braced himself grimly, knowing that it would do no good to lie about Major Williard's confidential orders. Even if he satisfied his captor that he was speaking the truth, it would mean a bullet in the head.

'Bring on yore redskins,' he grated, pulling in a hard breath. 'I won't tell nothin' to a man who's such a coward he's afraid to let his face be seen.'

He heard his captor rise from a squat and cross a short length of hard earthen floor. Cold night wind fanned the Rio Kid's face, followed by the sound of a door closing on bullhide hinges. Then the sound of retreating footsteps died away outdoors.

CHAPTER FIVE

MODOC CHIEFTAINS

Jerking his head backward and forward, Bob Pryor rubbed the knot of his blindfold against the rough bark wall at his back. Luck rewarded him with a protruding sliver which caught the fabric of the blindfold, enabling him to work it down over his nose.

He opened his eyes to find himself squinting into the glare of a stub of tallow candle jutting from the neck of a beer bottle which rested on an empty box a few feet in front of him.

Staring about, the Rio Kid saw that he had been brought to a small, pole-rafter cabin roughly ten feet square, and completely unfurnished. A square of scraped wolfskin formed a semitransparent window in the log wall opposite the slab door.

His feet were bound with hempen rope, knotted so securely that the Rio Kid gave up any attempt to wriggle free.

But another idea came to his fertile brain. Hitching himself across the earthen floor, he raised his hobnail-booted feet over the guttering candle flame, letting the fire kindle the strands of the rope trussing his legs.

The dry hemp charred. Heat blistered his calves. The rancid odor of his burning logboots wafted to his nostrils. It was a desperate race against time, for Pryor did not doubt that his captor would soon return with two Indians, bent on torturing him until he had betrayed Major Williard's secret plans for his conquest of the Lavabeds.

After an eternity of balancing his legs over the tiny flame, the Rio Kid felt the ropes part and he was able to kick his feet free. Then, rolling over on his side, he leaned against the sputtering candle and set to work burning his arm bonds in two.

Ten minutes dragged like an eon before the dry cordage parted and he was tugging his arms free, pulling off the ropes which coiled about him.

The last rope fell to the floor just as the Rio Kid's ears caught a mutter of voices outside. He saw the hickory bar of the slab door jerk taut as a hand pulled the latch string outside.

Sweat burst from the Texan's pores as he realized that the Indians had trapped him. The skin-covered window was barely a foot square, too small for escape. His hands flashed to his holsters, found them empty. His bowie knife had been removed from its sheath.

A wild glance around the cabin told him that no weapon was available. And the slab door was beginning to swing open!

In the clock-tick of time remaining to him, the Rio Kid stooped to pinch out the stub of candle and seize the quart beer bottle by the neck, snatching at the only weapon at his command. The door swung open, revealing the silhouetted figures of two squatty Indians whose jutting eagle feathers identified them as Modoc chieftains.

The cabin was in pitch blackness. The two Modocs paused a moment on the threshold, letting their eyes become accustomed to the dark. They muttered between themselves in their native jargon, apparently suspecting nothing wrong in the sudden extinguishing of the candle. The blast of wind from the opening door could have accounted for that.

One of the Modocs groped into the cabin, fumbling in his linsey-woolsey shirt for matches. His companion waited in the doorway, silhouetted against the winking lights of Stateline down the mountain slope.

Pryor pounced then with all the ferocity of a

cougar, and swung the beer bottle in a sweeping arc toward the nearest Modoc's head. The glass clubbed against the Indian's pate and exploded in a spray of shards. The Modoc slumped sideward, dazed by the terrific blow.

*   *   *

Vaulting his adversary's sprawling body, Pryor launched himself at the Indian on the threshold, wielding the jagged stub of bottle like a knife. The notched fangs of the broken bottle raked down the Indian's cheek as the Modoc fell back, bawling with pain. Blood showered Pryor as he followed the slashing stroke with a left uppercut that landed home on a jutting chin with all the power in the man's husky arm.

Knocked spinning, the Indian sprawled outside and measured his length on the ribbon of path leading to the cabin. Pryor leaped to follow up his momentary advantage, then tripped over the first Indian's legs and sprawled through the doorway.

He had a dim glimpse of the other chieftain scrambling to his feet, groaning with pain. Then, without waiting to give battle, the Indian whirled and bolted into the underbrush, crashing through the trees in desperate, headlong flight.

Panting heavily, the Rio Kid came to his

feet, stepping back into the cabin and straining his ears. The groaning of the Modoc at his feet and the far-off sounds of revelry and street traffic down in Stateline were the only noises he could identify.

The white man who had questioned him, then, had not returned with 'Hooker Jim' and 'Boston Charley.' But he might show up at any moment, and he would be armed.

Closing the door of the cabin, the Rio Kid struck a match, found the candle and lighted it.

The Modoc—whether he was Hooker Jim or Boston Charley, the Kid could not tell—was showing signs of returning consciousness. The Rio Kid's first move was to take possession of a pair of matched Colt .45s which the Indian had jabbed in his belt.

The heft of the weapons informed Pryor, even before he examined them closely, that they were his own guns! In all probability, then, this Indian and his companion had been the ones who had attacked him in the rear of the Golden Poppy Saloon and brought him up the slope to this prospector's deserted shack.

Using the rope which had bound him, the Rio Kid hogtied the groaning Indian hand and foot. He debated whether to question the Modoc, on the off chance that the Indian spoke English, concerning the identity of the white man who, in some fashion, knew of the Rio Kid's assignment from Major Williard.

Then, realizing the danger of letting himself be trapped a second time, he slipped out into the night. He concealed himself in the brush a dozen yards from the shack, where he could spot his mysterious inquisitor coming up the trail.

Twenty minutes passed without any sign of the other Indian's return. The Rio Kid finally plotted out a course of action. He would escort his Indian captive back to Stateline and turn him over to Sergeant Walker Henry for transfer back to Major Williard's headquarters. The Army would regard any sub-chieftain of Captain Jack's as a fine prize of war.

In the act of emerging from the undergrowth and returning to the cabin, Bob Pryor's attention was arrested by a thud of hoofs moving up the slope to his rear. At first thought, he believed that his questioner was returning to the cabin with a group of confederates, all mounted. If so, it would be out of the question to challenge such overwhelming odds.

Crouching low in the tangled thicket, the Rio Kid wriggled his way through the brush in the direction of the approaching cavalcade. Then he was peering out over a broad trail which he recognized as the one he had traveled to reach Stateline a few hours before.

Almost abreast of his hiding place was a single mounted man, dressed in mackinaw and

43

floppy-brimmed hat, riding a mule of such diminutive stature that the rider's legs nearly scraped the ground. Following the mule rider was a string of pack horses, each loaded with a pair of heavy wooden crates diamond-hitched to the packsaddles.

Obviously, this was a pack train outbound from Stateline with trade goods. And they were heading in the direction of the Modoc-held Lavabeds!

* * *

Starlight gleaming on the white-painted boxes revealed large fleur-de-lis designs stenciled on their sides, together with large printed letters: 'Consigned to Bon Marche Warehouse, Stateline.' This mule train, then, belonged to Dorian Fiske!

The rider halted his mule directly opposite the spot where the Rio Kid crouched in the ailanthus thicket above the trail, and struck a match to light his corncob pipe. The flare of light behind the mule-skinner's cupped palms revealed a craggy, whiskery-faced man whom the Rio Kid remembered having seen at the bar of the Golden Poppy.

His pipe spouting tiny bomb-bursts of smoke, the man jerked on his lead rope and headed on up the trail, moving out of range of the Rio Kid's vision.

Questions hammered at Pryor's aching

skull. Was it customary for Dorian Fiske to send his pack trains out into Indian-infested timberland in the dead of night? Did Fiske have some reason for the secrecy which seemed to enshroud the departure of this mule string from Stateline?

'Ten to one it's a shipment headed for Captain Jack's holin'-in place,' Pryor muttered. 'If it is, then Riddle's hunch about Fiske workin' in league with the Modocs was correct.'

Trailing the pack mules would be simple, even on foot. But he had the Indian chieftain in the cabin to think about. It would not do to let his captive be rescued by his Indian companion or by anyone else hostile to the Army.

Pryor headed back through the brush toward the cabin, fuming with impatience. If only Celestino were on hand to take over the Indian's custody, leaving him free to trail the suspicious-looking pack train toward the Lavabeds!

Bob Pryor pushed open the door of the cabin where he had been held prisoner. The candle was still burning on the dirt floor of the shack. But the Indian he had left here less than half an hour ago was gone.

A pile of cut ropes lay on the cabin floor. And it was impossible that the Modoc could have freed himself!

Then a glance at the knife-ripped window

on the opposite wall told the Rio Kid what had happened. The Indian's fellow-chief had wriggled through the narrow opening to rescue his partner, perhaps during the time Pryor had been keeping the cabin under close watch from the Stateline trail.

CHAPTER SIX

TRAIL TO TRAGEDY

Any attempt to track down the fugitive Modocs would be a fruitless waste of time in this brushy terrain and in the darkness, the Rio Kid concluded. Waiting for the white man to show up at the cabin might also be futile. The fact that he had not re-turned with Boston Charley and Hooker Jim was proof that he expected the Indians to report to him at some other rendezvous, following their torture and slaying of their prisoner.

Cursing at the opportunity which had slipped through his fingers, Pryor headed back down the slope toward Stateline. Reaching the edge of the town, he consulted his watch in the glare of a miner's lighted window.

It was a little after midnight. More time had elapsed when he was unconscious than he had estimated, for it had been shortly after ten o'clock when he had left the Golden Poppy.

Avoiding the main street, Pryor searched out the Cascades Livery Barn down by the river, where Winema had suggested that Celestino wait. He found his young Mexican friend playing monte with the hostlers. Celestino excused himself and joined the Rio Kid outside the livery barn.

The ugly blue welt on Pryor's temple required explanations. Tersely the Rio Kid outlined the events that had transpired since his arrival in Stateline four hours before.

'Saber is hitched in front of the Golden Poppy, Celestino,' the Rio Kid wound up. 'It wouldn't do for me to pick him up. I'll take yore mustang and meet yuh at the head of the trail leadin' into town. *Andale*, amigo. We can't run the risk of losin' track of Fiske's mule string.'

Mireles grinned, eager for action following his long period of waiting at the livery stable for his partner's arrival.

'My black is saddled and waiting, General,' he whispered. 'I weel breeng heem pronto.'

In a short time the Rio Kid was heading out of Stateline astride Celestino's powerful midnight black stallion. By the time he reached the head of the Lavabeds trail, his Mexican partner was approaching on Saber, Pryor's leggy dun.

They switched mounts and headed on up the trail into the sugar pines, riding abreast as they passed the spot where the Rio Kid had

47

spied on Fiske's mule driver.

A tardy moon gave them ample light to follow the winding trail when they were an hour out of Stateline. So far they had not overhauled Fiske's pack train, but the tracks of the mules were plain on the well-traveled trail, proof that the muleteer had not cut off onto some obscure game trail en route.

They reached a fork in the trail an hour later and dismounted to read sign. The Rio Kid's pulses raced as he saw that Dorian Fiske's mule train had left the main route which led to Yreka and the scene of Jed Blake's massacre. Instead, the heavily-loaded mules had turned southeast, following a deer trail which headed in the general direction of Tule Lake and the Lavabeds.

'I think we're follerin' a good hunch here, Celestino,' Pryor commented, as they remounted. 'Freight traffic usually keeps to the main road headed south. There ain't any settlement east of here, accordin' to Williard. Which means that Fiske's merchandise is headed either to the Army post or the Injun country over in the Lavabeds.'

They pushed off down the deer trail, loosening their six-guns in holsters. Fiske's mules could not be far ahead, plodding at their slow gait. When once they had spotted the mule string, they planned to trail at a safe distance. Daylight should find them at the edge of the Lavabeds, where they could get positive proof that Dorian Fiske was dealing with the Modocs.

Then, without warning, there came to the ears of the two man hunters a sharp fusillade of gunfire, somewhere beyond the ridge they were climbing. The shooting trailed off, followed by blood-curdling Indian war whoops, then a brooding silence broken only by the sough of the night wind through the lofty sugar pines.

*   *   *

The Rio Kid and Celestino reined up staring at each other.

'Sounds like the Modocs jumped Fiske's mule drover!' Pryor exclaimed, hauling his carbine from its boot under the saddle fender. 'If that's the case, we were mistaken about where that freight shipment was headed, Celestino.'

They galloped to the top of the rise and dipped into the ravine beyond. The trail led down into a rocky canyon where a tributary of Lost River drained into Tule Lake, the latter body of water visible in the distance, its mirror-smooth surface dancing with moonbeams.

Beyond Tule Lake loomed the forbidding reaches of the Lavabeds, domain of the warring Modocs.

'No use riskin' our own scalps, Celestino!'

49

Pryor whispered, stepping out of saddle. 'We'll hide our mounts and go on afoot. That shootin' didn't come from far up that canyon.'

Leaving Saber and the Mexican's stallion ground-hitched in a brushy defile well off the trail, the two partners headed on down the trail, rifles ready for emergencies.

Before they reached the burbling torrent at the pit of the canyon, they heard a rumble of hoofs heading in the direction of the Lavabeds, accompanied by triumphant Indian shouts. Then a bend in the canyon cut off the megaphoning noises.

Sprinting down the trail, the Rio Kid suddenly flung out an arm to halt his Mexican *companero.* Celestino spotted the sprawled figure in buckskins lying across the moonlit trail at the same instant.

It was the mule drover from the Bon Marche, the corncob pipe still clamped in his teeth. Feather-tipped arrows jutted from the skinner's mackinaw and he had been riddled with ambush lead. There was no trace of the mule train or its cargo.

White-faced and tense, Bob Pryor and Celestino approached the prostrate figure. It seemed impossible that Fiske's drover could be alive, but as they drew closer they saw a jet of tobacco smoke fork from the man's nostrils.

Riddled with bullets, bristling with arrows, the muleskinner was smoking his way into eternity!

The man's eyes fluttered open as the Rio Kid knelt beside him, Celestino Mireles posting himself to one side with eyes raking the moon-drenched canyon beyond.

'Modocs jumped yuh, old-timer?' Pryor asked gently.

The corncob pipe waggled in the dying man's teeth as he struggled to speak.

'Yeah. Some skunk tipped off the red devils—I was slippin' out of—Stateline after dark. Dozen-odd—redskins—lyin' in wait choused my cargo.'

The Rio Kid leaned closer to catch the drover's whispered words. A death rattle was in the man's throat and any moment might be his last on earth.

'Is Dorian Fiske workin' with the Modocs?' Pryor demanded tensely. 'Try and talk, *amigo*. We're friends.'

The mule driver's body shook with a paroxysm of agony. Crimson bubbles swelled and broke on the corners of his mouth as the pipe dropped from his lips.

'My cargo—blankets an' pup tents—for Williard's Army,' the drover got out. 'Cap'n Jack—uh—ahhh—'

The man's whisper trailed off and his eyes rolled gruesomely in their sockets as his mortal spirit took wing.

The Rio Kid came to his feet, tugging off his coonskin cap and staring down at the dead man.

'I don't know what to make of this, Celestino,' he said bleakly. 'He didn't say yes or no about Fiske dealin' with the Modocs. On the face of it, I'd say that tonight's attack shows Dorian Fiske ain't guilty. After all, we only had Frank Riddle's hunch to go on.'

Celestino reached out to seize his partner's sleeve, pointing with his rifle barrel in the direction from which they had come.

'*Caballos*—horses come, General!' the Mexican whispered. 'Indians, perhaps. We hide, *no es verdad?'*

*　　　*　　　*

Vaulting the muleskinner's corpse, the Rio Kid and Celestino leaped off the trail and scrambled down into the glacial boulders which rimmed the mountain stream.

They had barely taken concealment when a cavalcade of mounted Indians galloped down the trail from the direction of Stateline, their ponies' hoofs trampling the dead freighter as they swept on down the canyon.

There were ten riders in all, and from his hiding place in the boulders the Rio Kid recognized at least two of the Modocs. One, his face wrapped in swathing bandages, was the Indian he had slashed with the broken beer bottle. The leader of the cavalcade was the Indian who had been rescued from the cabin before midnight. Boston Charley and Hooker

52

Jim.

But the moonlight also had revealed the identity of two riders who were roped to their saddles. Even after the Indians had thundered past and vanished around the curving gorge, the Rio Kid wondered if his imagination had been playing him tricks. It had seemed to him, in the fleeting glimpse he had had of the Modocs' prisoners, that they were—

'Frank Riddle an' hees *esposa*, Senora Winema!' gasped Celestino, confirming Bob Pryor's identification. 'Thos' Indios captured our *amigos* over een Stateline, no?'

Horror coursed through the Rio Kid's veins as he realized what had transpired. Two days ago, Captain Jack had launched a surprise attack on Blake's Farm with the idea of wreaking his vengeance against his blood cousin, Winema, and her white husband, Frank Riddle.

The Lion of the Lavabeds had been thwarted in his designs at Blake's by the timely intervention of the Rio Kid and Celestino Mireles. But Captain Jack had not delayed long in striking again at the young squaw who was serving as an interpreter for the U.S. Army.

'This accounts for Boston Charley's and Hooker Jim's presence near Stateline last night, Celestino!' the Rio Kid exclaimed. 'They must have known where the Riddles were stayin' and kidnaped 'em! Major Williard says that Captain Jack placed a bounty on the topknots of Winema and her husband.'

Of one accord, the two adventurers climbed out of the rocks and headed up the trail where they had left Saber and the black stallion. They did not speak again until they were in saddle, heading down the canyon trail in pursuit of the Indian band.

Their horses shied in passing the hoof-mangled corpse of Dorian Fiske's mule-skinner, but there was no time to waste in burying the unfortunate man. Much as it went against the Rio Kid's grain to leave a fellow white man as prey for coyotes and buzzards, the plight of Winema and Frank Riddle demanded their utmost efforts.

'Half of our job is to scout the Lavabeds and give the Army an idea of the strength of Captain Jack's forces,' Pryor called to the Mexican who galloped at his stirrup. 'We know them redskins are headed for the Lavabeds. This is our chance to find the trail to Captain Jack's hidin' place!'

That they were heading, two white men, into a tangled *malpais* of treeless rocks and bottomless canyons where hostile Modocs had kept a formidable U.S. Army at bay for months, did not deter Pryor and Celestino now.

The Modocs were notorious for their torture of helpless prisoners, and both men knew that Captain Jack would reserve his most excruciating punishment for Winema and her husband. In the Modocs' eyes, the young squaw was guilty of treason to her race, and the fact that she was being taken alive into the Lavabeds was proof that Captain Jack demanded personal retribution against his cousin!

CHAPTER SEVEN

INTO THE LAVABEDS

Dawn was staining the lofty volcanic formations of the Lavabeds when the trailing avengers caught sight of the Indian band led by Hooker Jim and Boston Charley. The cavalcade was traveling at a slower gait now, threading along the rimrock which overhung the cold waters of Tule Lake.

'We can never hope to foller 'em into the Lavabeds on hossback, Celestino,' the Rio Kid said dubiously. 'We'd be picked off from ambush within a mile. I'm afraid we've got to turn our *caballés* loose to graze until we can come back for 'em, *compadre.*'

They reined off into the sparse timber which lined the north shore of Tule Lake and stripped saddles from Saber and the black, caching their gear and bridles in a leafy maple, well off the ground where rodents would not damage the leather.

Both men choked with emotion as they turned their prime saddlers loose to graze. Neither confessed to the other the feeling that was uppermost in their minds—that they might not live to reclaim the two saddlers. In such an eventuality, at least the horses were free to forage for themselves.

Leaving their rifles behind and carrying only a saddlebag loaded with provisions and a canteen of water, they pushed on down the trail which entered the northern reaches of the Lavabeds.

Within the space of a hundred yards, it seemed that they had invaded the sterile Mountains of the Moon. All trace of trees and grass and wild mountain flowers were left behind at the edge of the vast scoria fields.

Following the captors of Winema and Frank Riddle was not difficult, for the lava held traces of passing hoofs. That indicated that the canyon they were following, while it held no clearly defined trail, was a commonly used route of travel for Indians coming from and going to the wild *pedregal* they had chosen for their last stand.

The sun had climbed to its noon position in the cloudless sky before the Rio Kid and Celestino Mireles came in sight of the Indians they were following. It was rough going for horses, and all of the Modoc party, with the exception of their two prisoners, were working their way into the Lavabeds on foot, leading their ponies.

The pursuers were traversing a dead, bitter land that defied description. One moment they were recoiling from yawning fissures in the volcanic rock which seemed to be bottomless cracks penetrating awesomely to the core of the earth; the next they were detouring around the bases of lofty cinder cones or towering chimney rocks which spiked the *pedregal* like mammoth stalactites.

Innumerable caves and eroded grottos stippled the layers of hardened lava. They chose one to rest in when hunger and fatigue overcame them, there wolfing down a hurried meal.

Then they were again resuming their trek, shivering one minute in blue-clotted shadow where the sun's rays never penetrated, and boiling the next where beetling igneous cliffs radiated the sunshine like the sides of a furnace.

It was two o'clock by Pryor's watch when, unexpectedly, they crawled out on a lofty ledge to find they had reached the end of the trail.

A sparkling artesian well gushed from a scarp-rimmed basin below them, fed by gravity from melting snowfields higher in the Siskiyous—the 'Fountain of the Gods' which Winema had reported as being the Modocs' water supply.

Beyond the geysering well was the entrance

of a mighty cavern which dwarfed the others Pryor and Mireles had seen. Modoc warriors thronged in and out of the cavern like ants.

They saw no trace of Hooker Jim and Boston Charley, but the horses they had been trailing into the Lavabeds were drinking at the rim of a pool beside the artesian well. From somewhere back in the dark confines of the cave came the pulsing throb of Modoc war drums, tom-tomming in celebration of the capture of Winema and her white husband.

'This,' the Rio Kid whispered, 'is the Modoc headquarters.'

*   *   *

Of Winema and Riddle they saw nothing. The prisoners had already been conducted inside the cavern which, the Rio Kid judged, was the headquarters camp of Captain Jack's band.

Remembering that Major Williard wanted a tally of Modoc strength, the two spies counted the assembled Indian braves as best they could and estimated them to number over three hundred—roughly half of the fighting population of the tribe, according to the Army's information.

'The others are scattered around the borders of the Lavabeds, on defense patrol,' the Rio Kid muttered. 'There are no squaws here, and that means that this is a military headquarters for the Modocs, Celestino. The old men and the women and kids must be camped somewhere else—further back in the Lavabeds probably, out of range of artillery fire.'

The young Mexican scanned the Indian throngs at the entrance of the cavern and shuddered involuntarily.

'Senora Winema and her *esposo*, they are the gone gooses, no?' he whispered. 'We can do nossings to safe them ageenst such odds, General.'

The Rio Kid nodded, sick with despair as he contemplated the fate which awaited the two interpreters. Perhaps at this moment, Captain Jack and his cohorts were indulging in savage rituals inside the cavern, meting out to Winema and Frank Riddle inhuman penalties for their 'treason.'

While the two men watched, they saw husky young braves move out of the cavern with the string of mules belonging to Dorian Fiske. Older bucks gathered around and the pack animals were butchered with dispatch, to provide meat for the beleaguered tribe.

Suddenly the skies were heavy with remote thunder, though not a cloud was visible. Celestino stiffened, touching the Rio Kid's arm and pointing off to the southwest.

Black puffs of smoke appeared in the sky, and the steady rumble of thunder increased in volume. The rocks where they lay seemed to vibrate to a remote concussion, as if an earthquake was convulsing the Lavabeds.

'Cannonadin'!' Pryor whispered. 'Williard has moved his howitzers up to try to shell the Modocs out into the open.'

Glancing around at the ugly vista of the Lavabeds, the Rio Kid smiled bleakly. Storming the Modoc stronghold with cannon was like assaulting an elephant with pea-shooters. The artillery did not exist which could make a dent on these upflung badlands.

'*Caramba!*' whispered Mireles. 'Thos' anthill has been tromped on by these cannon fire, General. Look!'

The Rio Kid swung his gaze back to the cave. The vast underground citadel was disgorging scores of warriors, carrying stolen Army rifles, and loaded down with belts of ammunition.

In their lead strode a powerful figure in buckskins, with a red-tipped eagle feather jutting from his bobbed hair.

'Captain Jack!' Pryor exclaimed. 'The soldiers have tromped on the Lion's tail, Celestino. He's afraid that the bombardment will mebbe mean a full-scale infantry assault.'

It was true. The Lion of the Lavabeds, shouting orders in the jargon of his tribe, was leading his warriors out into the tangled volcanic wilderness, heading in the direction of the howitzer attack. If Major Williard backed his cannoneers with infantry, they would meet a withering defensive fire.

Within ten minutes, the scene was deserted except for one white-haired old warrior who was busy cutting steaks from the skinned carcasses of the mules, down by the artesian fountain.

'It's almost as if Major Williard timed that artillery attack to draw Captain Jack's forces away from here, Celestino!' whispered the Rio Kid exultantly. 'Now's our chance, if ever, to rescue Winema and Riddle! And do a little explorin' while we're at it.'

Fierce lights glinted in Celestino's black eyes. He was like a war horse responding to the bugle ordering a charge.

'There weel be guards een the *cueva*,' he warned. 'And *quizas*—perhaps the preesoners are already dead. Let's go, General!'

Cautiously, the two avengers began their silent trek down the lava slope toward the Fountain of the Gods. Miles to southward batteries of American guns were pounding the Lavabeds with shot and shell, unaware of the providential cover they were giving the two spies in the heart of the Modoc domain . . .

* * *

A circle of guttering pine-knot torches set in the cavern floor illuminated the vast, high-domed council chamber inside the Modoc cave. Frank Riddle, tied to a snubbing post imbedded in the lava paving, felt dwarfed by the vastness of the gallery.

His wife, Winema, had told him of the 'Great Cave' in the Lavabeds, having visited this awesome place in her girlhood when her father, the tribal medicine man, had visited the forbidden region to commune with the Modoc deities.

Winema had pictured the Great Cave as large enough to hide Mount Shasta. That was a girlish exaggeration, but Riddle knew that the subterranean room he was now in was double the size of the Mammoth Cave, back in his native Kentucky.

Unlike the latter, however, this cavity under the Lavabeds had no stalagmites depending from the ceiling, there being no limestone or dripping water in this barren terrain. This vast underground hall was a good two hundred yards from daylight, and but one of a number of labyrinthian passages.

The firelight did not penetrate to the rest of the cave, but Riddle knew that the Indians stabled their horses further back inside the mountain.

This was the council chamber, the spot set aside for the torture rituals accompanying the war dances where prisoners were burned at the stake. More than one Army picket had been kidnapped and brought here to die in agony, Riddle knew.

More than one of Major Williard's outriders and scouts had vanished without trace during the past winter, and Riddle did not doubt but that they had wound up even as he was, tied to a torture stake in Captain Jack's Great Cave.

Just inside the extreme reaches of the firelight, the bearded interpreter could see stacks of supplies which had been smuggled to the Modocs from the outside. Barrels of gunpowder, crates of Army blankets and other quartermaster goods plundered from military wagon trains in Oregon; vast quantities of foodstuffs, obtained from sources unknown to the high command.

Seeing the secret of Captain Jack's strength, Riddle doubted if the Modoc War would ever be won by the whites. It would end in a stalemate, with Captain Jack and his son's sons reigning supreme as kings of the Lavabeds.

At the far side of the cavern, Winema was roped to another torture stake. A pair of armed Modoc sentries, young braves with half-healed battle wounds had been left behind to maintain a guard over the prisoners.

When today's battle was over and Captain Jack's weary legions trooped back to the Great Cave, there would be a debauch in which Winema and Riddle would play the chief roles—human torches.

Riddle had been without hope, ever since the evening before when he and his Indian wife had been captured by Modocs who had surrounded their little cabin in Stateline and kidnapped them without attracting the attention of neighbors. It had been a daring coup of Captain Jack's, sending Modoc warriors into the paleface settlement and seizing them without detection.

For himself, Riddle had no fear of torture and death. It was the price he must pay for the love he had known for the beautiful Indian girl who had become his wife. But he would have pawned his chances of heaven to be able to put a merciful bullet through Winema's brain and spare her the hideous death which her cousin, the Modocs' Lion of the Lavabeds, was holding in store for her.

He called his wife's name, but she did not stir. She hung limply in the ropes which bound her to the torture stake across the cavern floor, head slumped on her chest, slumbering from the rigors of the grueling trail ride of the night past.

As the echoes of his voice reverberated through the great lava-arched gallery, Riddle heard a commotion at the entrance of the gallery. Twisting his head around, the interpreter stared in the direction of the two guards who patrolled the grotto.

Riddle's jaw sagged open as he saw that one of the guards was sprawled on his back, the haft of a bowie knife jutting from his naked chest. And the other guard was wrestling in the grip of a buckskin-clad white man!

'Rio Kid!'

Riddle gasped the name even as he saw

64

Captain Bob Pryor wrest a carbine from the struggling Indian and smash the butt hard to the Modocs' temple, His skull crushed by the clubbing rifle stock, the second guard slumped and lay motionless at Pryor's feet.

CHAPTER EIGHT

DEN OF THE LION

Riddle struggled to speak, but his throat seemed paralyzed. He saw Celestino emerge from behind a fluted column of lava from which the Mexican had flung his knife at the unsuspecting Indian sentry, to join the Rio Kid at the edge of the glow of pine torches which shed their ruddy witch-glow over the vast cavern.

'Pryor! Pryor!' the interpreter shouted, finding speech at last. 'It's all right! If you've taken care of the outer guards you have no more Indians to worry about!'

Winema lifted her head and stared in disbelief as, roused from her stupor by her husband's shout, she watched Celestino Mireles and the Rio Kid race over to the stake where Riddle was awaiting torture.

A knife blade flickered in the gloom and then her husband was seizing the bowie from the Rio Kid's hand and racing across the cavern toward her. For the first time in their married years together, Winema gave way to feminine sobs as Riddle slashed her bonds and gathered her in his arms.

The Indian girl was drying her eyes when Bob Pryor and his Mexican partner, their faces wreathed with grins in the firelight, approached them across the cavern floor.

'You saved us from unspeakable doom, Captain,' choked Frank Riddle, his own eyes swimming. 'Winema and I are forever in your debt!'

The Rio Kid accepted his knife from the interpreter and slid it into its sheath. His face sobered, now that the exultation of their successful entry into the Great Cave was completed.

'We've got to get out of here, fast,' he said. 'The American cannonadin' is finished. Captain Jack and his band will come back here. And we'll have every Modoc in the Lavabeds combin' the place for us.'

Winema reached out to clutch the Rio Kid's buckskin sleeve.

'I know these Lavabeds,' she panted hoarsely. 'I can lead you quickly to safety. I show you with a diagram—Watch!'

Pryor scowled curiously as he saw the Indian girl go down on one knee to trace a design in the dust with a finger tip.

'This is Tule Lake,' the girl said, drawing a crude oblong. 'Here'—scratching a wavy line

66

away from the Lake—'is the gorge which carries the water from the Fountain of the Gods into Tule Lake. The Modocs call it Flintridge Canyon. It opens on Tule Lake through a tiny break in the cliffs which my tribe calls *lauisis*, or the Devil's Eve. It is not visible from Elkorn's place on the far shore.'

The girl laid a lava pebble at the end of the crooked line.

'This rock,' she explained, 'is the Great Cave, my cousin Kintupash's headquarters. From the mouth of this cavern we can see where the Fountain drains into the head of Flintridge Canyon. Within an hour's time we can be at the edge of Tule Lake within swimming distance of Miles Elkorn's sawmill on the west shore!'

The Rio Kid helped Winema to her feet.

'*Bueno*,' he said crisply. 'Celestino, you and the Riddles get started for the canyon. I'll foller. But while I'm here, I've got to check on the trade goods Captain Jack has stored here. If I'm not mistaken they'll prove to be the main supply dump that Major Williard wanted me to locate.'

Mireles bent a nervous stare at his partner.

'You weel not tarry long, General?' he asked anxiously. 'Your life weel not be worth a *peseta* eef *Capitàn* Jack and hees *Indios* catch you here.'

Pryor waved impatiently toward the exit of the vast chamber, guarded now by the corpses of the guards they had stalked in the outer grotto.

'Get a move on!' he ordered harshly. 'Them barrels are full of gunpowder, if I ain't mistaken. I don't want to miss a chance to wipe out Captain Jack's arsenal at one fell swoop.'

*   *   *

Celestino scowled indecisively, then followed Winema and Frank Riddle toward the exit of the Great Cave. The Rio Kid strode rapidly toward the supply cache, pausing when he reached the stack of gunpowder barrels.

Some of the crates bore the insignia of the Army's quartermaster corps. Others displayed the fleur-de-lis insignia of Dorian Fiske's Bon Marche Warehouse in Stateline. Here, the Rio Kid realized, was probably the concentration point for the smuggled supplies which unknown renegades had delivered to the Lion of the Lavabeds.

Even if he lost his life in the destruction of this supply dump, the Rio Kid believed it worth the gamble. The backbone of Captain Jack's resistance would be shattered if his store of ammunition, food and blankets was destroyed.

Rolling one of the oaken powder kegs away from the pile, Pryor kicked the barrel head until one slat gave way, spilling out a heap of black gunpowder.

Working with feverish haste, Pryor rolled the broken barrel over to the tiers of supply cases, making sure that the scattered gunpowder was in an unbroken heap. Then, rolling the barrel ahead of him, the Rio Kid trailed a line of gunpowder across the gallery floor and into the exit tunnel where the corpses of the Modoc guards lay stiffening.

The gunpowder was exhausted by the time the Rio Kid was halfway to the vast arch of daylight marking the mouth of Captain Jack's headquarters.

He was racing against time. Any moment might see the return of the Modocs, in which case he would be trapped without hope of escape. But the end result seemed to justify the risk.

Hurrying back inside the main cavern, the Rio Kid broke open another barrel of gunpowder and dumped it thoroughly around the stores. That done, he walked over to one of the guttering pine-knot torches which formed a ring around the center of the cavern and tugged it from its socket in the lava floor.

The pitch-laden torch trailed a feather of black smoke behind the buckskin-clad Army scout as he hurried toward the mouth of the cave. When he had reached the end of his line of spilled gunpowder, the Rio Kid halted.

He sized up the amount of space he had to cover to reach daylight. Through the open maw of the cave, past the sprawled body of the mule butcher whom Celestino had dropped with a hard-flung knife, he saw the looming mouth of a canyon which he judged would be the Flintridge, leading to Tule Lake and safety, carrying off the surplus waters of the sparkling Fountain of the Gods.

With a muttered prayer for the success of his plan, Bob Pryor dropped his flaming torch on the gunpowder. The black grains ignited with a blinding *whoosh* and a writhing snake of red fire began racing down the spilled trail of powder. When it reached the stacked barrels of explosive there would be a blast of earth-shattering violence.

Spinning on his heels, the Rio Kid sprinted down the cavern and out into the blinding sunlight. He was halfway across the open ground in front of the Great Cave when he was flung off his feet by a shattering detonation which seemed to split the whole earth to its very core.

Swallowing the initial blast of the detonating gunpowder there came a louder, more terrible roar of sound numbing the Rio Kid's eardrums and shaking the ground under him.

As he dragged himself shakily to his feet, his body dashed by the spray of the artesian well, he saw the great arched mouth of the cave fracture slowly, then collapse inward as tons of loose, decomposed lava gave way under the impact of the mighty concussion in the bowels of the earth.

Within the space of an eye-wink, the gouting cloud of powder smoke spewing from the entrance of Captain Jack's hideout was stoppered up for all time by the collapse of the cavern roof. Grinning exultantly, the Rio Kid turned and headed at a run for the mouth of Flintridge Canyon.

Waiting for him were Winema and Frank Riddle and Celestino, who had witnessed the success of the Rio Kid's daring coup.

*   *   *

The details of their wild flight down Flintridge Canyon's twisting course remained forever hazy in the memories of the four fugitives. Sunset glare was in their eyes when they finally emerged on the tule-bordered shore of the lake, wading out through the tiny opening of the Devil's Eye.

For a moment the Rio Kid experienced a pang of despair, believing that they faced a watery trap. High obsidian cliffs, glittering like black glass in the expiring rays of daylight, fell obliquely to the rippling waters of Tule Lake as far as the eye could reach to north and south.

It was Winema who pointed out the big pine snag which was floating in the tules at water's edge, and explained that the log could be made to serve as a crude raft to carry them to the western shore where a column of smoke lifted from the site of Miles Elkorn's sawmill camp.

'Let's get goin',' Bob Pryor said anxiously. 'I think I see now where this terrible Modoc War can be finished off in a hurry. I've got to reach Mayor Williard's headquarters as quickly as I possibly can!'

*   *   *

Major Tracy Williard sat in his headquarters tent on the rim of the Lavabeds, poring over his campaign maps by the light of a lantern suspended from the ridge pole. His heart was heavy tonight. Before him were the reports of the artillery commander who had laid a barrage on what they believed to be Captain Jack's headquarters throughout the afternoon.

But scouting parties, visiting the target before sundown, had returned with the discouraging news that the attack had accomplished nothing. The campfire smokes which they thought marked the site of a Modoc encampment had turned out to be mere bonfires, set to draw the Americans' fire.

Williard looked up as his adjutant entered the tent, face flushed with excitement.

'The Rio Kid is outside with Miles Elkorn, sir,' the adjutant said after they had exchanged salutes. 'He says he brings urgent news,

Major.'

The old veteran of Gettysburg pushed aside his scriber and pencils and gestured vaguely.

'Send him in, Lieutenant. I must say I didn't expect to see Captain Pryor so soon, if ever.'

The buckskin-clad Texan entered, and at a signal pulled up a chair in front of Major Williard's field desk. Miles Elkorn, the Yankee sawyer, remained in the background.

'Major, I've just returned from the Lavabeds!' the Rio Kid said earnestly. 'Yuh'll pardon me if I sound like I'm boastin', and me a junior officer, but I believe I know a plan which will crush the Modoc defense and bring this campaign to an early end without a heap of losses for our side.'

Major Williard listened in growing amazement as the Rio Kid recounted the rescue of Winema and Frank Riddle, the discovery of the Modocs' water supply in the Fountain of the Gods, and the total destruction of Captain Jack's supply depot in the recesses of the Great Cave.

Snatching up a pencil, Pryor sketched a map similar to the one which Winema had drawn in the dust of the Great Cave's floor.

'My plan is this, sir,' the Rio Kid said excitedly. 'Winema says that the Modocs don't guard Flintridge Canyon, believin' that Tule Lake makes it impossible to reach from the outside. But yuh could ferry a right big body of troops across Tule Lake under cover of

73

darkness, and then—'

As the Rio Kid outlined his plan, Major Williard's gaunt features took on new hope. The way Pryor outlined his strategy, it seemed as workable as it was daring.

Troops filtering through the narrow opening of Devil's Eye could, with a minimum risk of detection, mass themselves within easy striking distance of the Fountain of the Gods, which was of necessity the focal point of Captain Jack's defense. Once their source of water was shut off by American soldiers, it would be only a question of time before the Modocs would be forced to surrender or make a break out of the Lavabeds. In that case they could be cut down by the troops which surrounded the area.

'Captain Jack is a prisoner in his own trap, Major,' the Rio Kid said earnestly. 'He wouldn't dream that your troops could invade the very heart of his stronghold till it would be too late!'

CHAPTER NINE

WAGONEER WANTED!

Major Williard tugged at his beard, dubious lights kindling in his red-shot eyes. He had listened thoughtfully to the Rio Kid.

74

'Your plan has but one drawback, Captain,' he said gravely when Pryor had finished. 'Judging from your report of the Modocs' strength, we'd need at least five hundred armed men to seize their water supply. That would not seriously drain my resources. But the question is—how could we secretly transport that many soldiers across a body of water as exposed as Tula Lake? How could my men reach this Devil's Eye you mention?'

The Rio Kid grinned, turning to motion Miles Elkorn up to the table.

'I've already fixed that,' he said. 'Elkorn here can build rafts at his sawmill and launch 'em in the lake within forty-eight hours. Next Wednesday night, accordin' to the almanac, the moon won't rise till midnight. Between sundown and eleven o'clock, Elkorn's rafts can cross the lake and unload five hundred men at the mouth of Flintridge Canyon. The rest is no more'n a matter of surprise attack on the defenders of the artesian well.'

Major Williard glanced up at the lumber baron to whom he already owed so much in material aid.

'Elkorn, I respect your mature judgment,' the officer said. 'What do you think of the Captain's scheme?'

Elkorn's pock-pitted face wreathed in smiles.

'I'm no military man, Major,' the sawmill man said, 'but to my way of thinking, the Rio

75

Kid has thought up a mighty fine scheme. I'd be willin' to wager everything I own that a week from now, yuh'll have pulled the fangs from yore Lion of the Lavabeds.'

Williard consulted his calendar.

'This is Sunday night,' he said. 'Pryor thinks Wednesday is the logical time to pull this surprise raid. Could you have enough rafts built to transport my personnel and their supplies by Wednesday afternoon, Elkorn?'

The sawmill man nodded emphatically.

'I guarantee it, sir. I can have the mill work day and night, if necessary, to turn out the required dimension lumber.'

'And the motive power for pulling the rafts across the Lake?'

Elkorn shrugged. 'I've got work boats I use for towin' logs to the mill. Twenty oars to the boat. My sawmill crew can provide the towin' power to land the rafts wherever yuh say. With a tail wind we should be able to cross Tule Lake inside of two hours.'

Major Williard got to his feet.

'Gentlemen,' he said, 'I shall issue the necessary orders at my end, if you will see to the construction of the rafts. I will summon in my staff officers and we'll hand-pick three companies of infantry to deliver the *coup de grace* to the Modocs.'

Despite the weariness which bogged at his muscles, Bob Pryor felt exhilarated as he and Miles Elkorn went out to where their saddle

76

horses were hitched.

'It galls the Major to see anybody he out-ranks come in from the outside and show him how to end this campaign, Kid,' Elkorn chuckled as they headed back toward the sawmill camp. 'Our advance word concernin' you hinted that yuh're somethin' of a genius. I, for one, am glad to admit it . . .'

With three full days stretching ahead before preparations could be completed for the secret attack on the Lavabeds, the Rio Kid spent Monday at the Army camp, resting. On Tuesday morning he borrowed a cavalry pony and rode to Stateline, where he booked a room in a frontier hotel overlooking Lost River.

Winema and Riddle had returned to Stateline the day before, escorted from Elkorn's camp by Sergeant Walker Henry and a platoon of cavalrymen instructed to protect the interpreters against a possible kidnap attempt by the Modocs and their accomplices.

*   *   *

Celestino Mireles had not been idle following their Sunday night crossing of Tule Lake on a floating log. He had snatched a few hours' rest at the sawmill and then had proceeded northward along the rim of Tule Lake to recover his black stallion and the Rio Kid's dun, Saber. The Mexican had stabled their horses at the Cascade before the Rio Kid's arrival in Stateline Tuesday noon.

The two partners chanced to meet on the main street, but gave no outward sign of recognition. Under the pretense of borrowing a match, the Rio Kid whispered to his Mexican comrade the name of the hotel where he had registered.

Pryor's reasons for not remaining at Williard's headquarters were vital ones. The identity of the renegades who had prolonged the Modoc War still remained unknown, and might remain so forever if the campaign should be mopped up before the week was over, as the Rio Kid hoped might be the case.

This meant that he had but forty-eight hours left in which to scout out clues to the source of the Modocs' smuggling ring. And Stateline seemed to be the logical starting point for such an undercover investigation. Despite the killing of the muleteer, the Rio Kid still included Dorian Fiske as a prime suspect.

That he was not engaged on a wildgoose chase, the Rio Kid was certain. The fact that he had been slugged and dragged up to the deserted shack on the hillside for questioning by an unknown white man was proof of that.

On the face of it, Pryor had reason to suspect that Dorian Fiske had been responsible for his kidnapping on the first night of his arrival in Stateline. But counteracting that line of reasoning was the fact that the Modocs had attacked one of Fiske's mule trains, bound to Major Williard's Army post with supplies, and had killed the muleskinner in charge. If Fiske were the trader guilty of smuggling trade goods into the Lavabeds, it did not seem logical that he would sacrifice a string of mules and one of his own employees to the Indians.

The Rio Kid returned to his hotel room at dusk after having spent the entire afternoon checking up on the various traders and freighting lines in Stateline. He found Celestino waiting for him, eyes flashing with excitement.

The Mexican was carrying a sheet of paper which, he said, he had torn off a bulletin board on the wall of the Golden Poppy Saloon when no one was looking.

'Thees may be important, General,' Celestino said. 'What you theenk, eh?'

The Rio Kid's lips moved silently as he read the bulletin:

WAGONEER WANTED!

The Bon Marche Warehouse has a Conestoga load of blasting powder consigned to a trading post at Jacksonville, Oregon, where it is urgently needed by settlers desiring to blast stumps from their farming lands along the Rogue River.

Owing to the danger of Indian attack in this territory and the impossibility of obtaining Army escorts for our wagons, the Bon Marche finds it impossible to hire a driver to transport the wagon into Oregon and deliver the load to its destination.

Anyone interested in this job should consult the undersigned without delay. Payment will be $500 in gold, $250 at time of leaving Stateline, balance payable on arrival in Jacksonville.

(signed) DORIAN FISKE, Prop. Bon Marche Warehouse

The Rio Kid glanced up to meet Celestino's flashing eyes, sharing the Mexican's excitement.

'It's a cinch that Fiske has reason to believe the Modocs have an eye on that wagon load of blastin' powder, Celestino!' Pryor exclaimed. 'Otherwise he wouldn't have any trouble hirin' one of his own wagoners to make that Jacksonville run! If he aims for that cargo to fall into Captain Jack's hands, it's plumb natural he'd want an outsider to drive the wagon. Then it wouldn't matter to Fiske if the driver was attacked and killed en route!'

Celestino nodded, grinning boyishly.

'That ees what I thought, General.'

'When did Fiske post this notice?' asked the Rio Kid.

Mireles plucked at the hem of his gaudy

serape. 'Not an hour ago, General. I stole thees paper almost as soon as he tacked it up, *es verdad.*'

*   *   *

Pryor paced the hotel room for a few moments, brows knitted in thought. Then he turned suddenly to his partner.

'Celestino, you're going to drive that load of blastin' powder out of Stateline tonight!' he said. 'And yuh're not goin' to risk losin' yore hair to a Modoc, either. I'll have Sergeant Henry and his platoon of cavalrymen meet yuh outside of town and hide in the wagon, just in case yuh're attacked!'

Celestino Mireles checked the loads in his six-guns and listened carefully as the Rio Kid outlined further details of his plan. As soon as the Kid had finished the Mexican was heading for the Golden Poppy Saloon to volunteer as a wagoneer in answer to Dorian Fiske's advertisement.

The Rio Kid hastened over to the shack on the outskirts of town where Frank Riddle and his Indian wife lived. He found the little cabin surrounded by a cordon of blue-coated cavalrymen, with Sergeant Walker Henry in charge. They had pitched their pup tents in the Riddle yard, making certain that the Modoc woman and her husband would be safe from possible kidnappers.

*　　*　　*

After conferring with Winema and Frank Riddle, the Rio Kid called the sergeant inside the cabin and outlined his plan.

'You select a squad of eight men to slip out of town after dark and wait for Celestino's wagon to show up on the Jacksonville road,' Pryor explained. 'Of course, my hunch may be wrong. Fiske may be on the up-and-up, about his trouble, what with drivers refusin' to take wagons out unescorted into the Indian country. On the other hand, if Fiske expects his blastin' powder to be grabbed by the Modocs before it gets to Jacksonville, you and yore men may get some target practice.'

Sergeant Henry, long since weary of routine garrison duty, rubbed his palms together excitedly. Then his face fell.

'But what if your Mexican friend doesn't land the job?' he inquired. 'Fiske might not want to hire a stranger.'

Pryor tongued his cheek thoughtfully.

'That's possible, of course. If so, I'll ride out myself and call yuh back, Sergeant. But Fiske has no way of knowin' that Celestino and I are workin' together. We've been careful not to be seen together here in Stateline. If Fiske is guilty, he'd hire anyone—just so's it wasn't one of his own wagoners.'

After Henry had gone out to pick men from

his platoon for the job ahead, Pryor turned to Riddle.

'I'll want you to keep a strict watch on Dorian Fiske's place this evenin',' he said. 'If yuh see Fiske leave town, especially if he appears to be follerin' Celestino's wagon, notify me right away. I'll be in my room in the El Dorado Hotel.'

CHAPTER TEN

ROUGE RIVER TRAPPERS

Walking back to the center of town, Bob Pryor was in time to see a canvas-hooded Conestoga drive out of the Bon Marche warehouse yard, with Celestino Mireles handling the six-horse team. After he had seen Celestino drive the wagon load of blasting powder across the river and disappear into the Oregon timber north of town, the Rio Kid ate a leisurely supper.

Plans were proceeding well. A mile up the road, Sergeant Walker Henry and his squad would board Fiske's wagon secretly. If Captain Jack's Modocs planned to intercept the Jacksonville wagon, they would receive a hot reception.

Pryor returned to the El Dorado Hotel and turned in early, satisfied that Frank Riddle would summon him in the event of anything suspicious on Dorian Fiske's part. He was sound asleep at midnight when he was awakened by a knock, urgently repeated.

Sliding out of bed, the Rio Kid reached under his pillow and drew out a six-gun, earing the hammer to full cock.

'Who is it?' he called softly.

'Riddle. I've got bad news for you, Captain.'

Pryor unlocked his door and admitted the bearded interpreter. The man was obviously in a state of high agitation, breathing so hard he found it difficult to speak.

Obeying Pryor's orders to keep watch on the Golden Poppy Saloon, Riddle had spotted Dorian Fiske leaving town by a back road around ten o'clock, taking great pains that his departure go unnoticed by the street throngs.

'Fiske headed up the trail which leads to the Lavabeds, instead of crossing the river as you expected he might,' Riddle said. 'Since he was on foot, I decided to trail him.' Riddle paused to recover his breath, ignoring the Rio Kid's nervous suspense. 'A mile out of town,' he went on then, 'Fiske was met by a group of Modocs. I recognized Schonchin and Boston Charley among them. I was able to get close enough to overhear their discussion. Dorian Fiske spoke the Modoc jargon better than I do. He's a quarter-breed.'

A sense of foreboding seized the Rio Kid, bringing a fine film of cold perspiration from his pores.

'Yes—go on!' he whispered impatiently. 'Why was Fiske havin' a secret confab with Captain Jack's lieutenants?'

Riddle came quickly to the point, and his report was dire in its potentialities of disaster:

'Fiske told the Indians that one of Miles Elkorn's lumberjacks had sneaked to town yesterday and told him that Major Williard plans a surprise attack on the Lavabeds before the moon rises on Wednesday night. The lumberjack said they were busy building rafts to ferry the soldiers across Tule Lake, to attack the Lavabeds through Flintridge Canyon.'

The Rio Kid blanched, dumbfounded by Riddle's words. Their closely guarded secret, shared by all the workmen in Elkorn's crew! And now in the possession of Captain Jack's hordes!

'Anyway,' Riddle went on before the Rio Kid could speak, 'Fiske said he had hired Celestino to drive a wagon load of blasting powder to Jacksonville, and he told Schonchin to attack the wagon and bring the powder back to the Lavabeds. The plan is to let Major Williard's men enter Flintridge Canyon, then they will blast down the walls of the gorge with Fiske's explosives, crushing the American soldiers to the last man!'

As Frank Riddle finished speaking, his silence was indicative that he shared Pryor's consternation.

With the Modocs warned well in advance of the strategy intended for their undoing, the whole plan was nipped in the bud.

The only good news Pryor could salvage from Riddle's report was confirmation of the fact that Dorian Fiske was guilty of a conspiracy with the warring Modocs.

There was plenty of time to call off the planned foray, thereby saving the lives of half a thousand hand-picked troopers. But of more immediate concern to the Rio Kid was the fact that Celestino's life was in danger. He had no way of knowing how many Indians would take part in the attack on the northbound wagon.

*   *   *

In all likelihood, the Modocs would attack the wagon with a sizable force, since possession of the blasting powder was important to their plans.

'Listen, Frank!' Bob Pryor exclaimed. 'I was thinkin' of ridin' down to Major Williard's and tellin' him to call off our plan for Wednesday night. But I think mebbe we may yet outwit the Modocs, thanks to yore good work tonight . . . What did Dorian Fiske do after he told the Indians of the blastin' powder shipment leavin' Stateline?'

Riddle shook his head despairingly.

'Fiske boarded Schonchin's pony and rode off with the Modocs,' he said. 'I couldn't follow. I thought it best to hurry back here and notify you what I had learned.'

Pryor's lips compressed grimly.

'Good!' he said. 'Now listen carefully, Riddle. We've got a chance to cook Fiske's goose and block Captain Jack's plans if we hurry. My plan is this—'

Lowering his voice almost to a whisper, the Rio Kid began to talk swiftly and earnestly . . .

Ten miles north of the California boundary, Celestino Mireles found himself faced by another bend of Lost River. He pulled up the Morgans at the edge of the freshet-swollen torrent and turned to peer through the puckered oval opening of the Conestoga.

Back in the gloom, squatting on the barrels of blasting powder which made up the mudwagon's cargo, Sergeant Walker Henry and twelve of his troopers were invisible in the darkness.

'Thees *rio*, she looks bad to cross at night, senor!' the Mexican said apprehensively. 'Do you know eef the ford ees safe een thees high water?'

The cavalry sergeant wriggled forward over the load and peered out at the rushing river, the stars reflected in its sluicing current.

'It's not as bad as it looks, Celestino,' Sergeant Henry reassured. 'I'd advise crossing. After all, Fiske gave you orders to travel all night and camp in the morning. Just keep to the ruts and head for those twin boulders on the far bank. I've seen smaller wagons than this one make the ford.'

Celestino shrugged and picked up his whip. The jouncing Conestoga splashed out into the stream and the Morgans surged ahead through belly-deep water, their hoofs finding solid footing on the gravel bed.

Icy water surged at the wagon box and spume dashed over the backs of the toiling team, but in a few moments the water shallowed perceptibly. The prairie schooner lurched up the north bank and followed the Jacksonville road out onto a grassy bench hemmed in by towering sugar pines.

A short distance beyond the river, the alert Mexican spotted a campfire twinkling against the background of the forest. Nerves on edge, Celestino whispered a warning for the cavalrymen inside the Conestoga to ready their guns for trouble.

Steering his team along the road which passed close to the campfire on its way into the forest, the Mexican saw two burly figures hunkered beside the fire, frying fish over the red coals. One of the campers got to his feet and strode out to meet the wagon, lifting an arm to the driver.

Loosening a six-gun in holster, Celestino braked the dripping Conestoga to a halt.

'Howdy,' greeted the bearded man. 'Yuh don't figger on goin' to Jacksonville with this mudwagon, do yuh?'

The Mexican thought fast. The question sounded innocent enough, but he would be in a predicament if these buckskin-clad men were looking for a ride north. He could not risk having anyone discover the presence of Sergeant Henry and his troopers hiding in the Conestoga.

'*Si*,' he answered uncertainly. '*Porque no—*why not?'

The trapper shook his head.

'My pardner and I just come from Jacksonville,' he said. 'Yuh can't make it. There's a bad rockslide up the road a piece. Yuh'll have to wait for daylight before yuh could shovel through. Take my word for it.'

*　　　*　　　*

Celestino muttered his thanks. This was a situation he had not anticipated. The trapper was obviously trying to help him.

'Tell yuh what, son,' the bearded man volunteered. 'Stop yore wagon on the bench yonder and graze yore team overnight. My name's Curt Condon and my pardner yander is Jeb O'Malley. We're trappers from the Rogue River country. Come daylight, we wouldn't mind ridin' up to the slide and lendin' a hand shovelin' a clear right-o'-way for yore wagon.'

Celestino Mireles gathered up his lines.

'*Muchas gracias*, Senor Condon,' he said. 'I weel camp here for the night as you say.'

Condon grinned.

'We got a mess of river trout fryin',' he said with bluff Western hospitality. 'Yuh're welcome to our vittles.'

Celestino sawed his lines and circled the wagon around toward the river, withdrawing fifty yards from the campfire before halting the Conestoga. With luck, he would be able to spend the night with the Rogue River trappers without them learning of the cavalrymen who rode as secret passengers in his wagon.

'Don't worry about us, Celestino!' whispered Sergeant Walker Henry from the hooded interior of the wagon. 'Me and my men will stand guard all night, in case any Injuns show up. You go ahead and eat a double portion of trout for us, eh?'

Celestino climbed down off the wagon and unhitched the horses. Stripping the harness from the Morgans, he ran a catch rope through their halters and headed off down the slope toward the river.

After watering his stock, the Mexican selected a patch of lush grass and set about picketing each of the Morgans for the night, picking up sticks and driving them into the turf with a rock.

He was heading back toward the hooded Conestoga when Curt Condon and Je O'Malley sauntered up to meet him.

'Ain't yuh afraid the redskins might sneak up durin' the night and try to run off yore team, son?' O'Malley asked. 'Yuh better stake 'em out between our campfire and the wagon.'

Celestino shook his head, hitching his gun-belts. A slight tremor of apprehension shot through him as he saw the two Rogue River trappers had moved to bracket his either elbow.

'I weel spread my bedroll nearby,' he said.

Celestino was caught unprepared for what happened next. Moving in unison, the buckskin-clad men lashed out legginged feet to trip the Mexican, throwing him heavily on his back. Before he could reach for a gun, Condon smashed him on the point of the jaw with the butt of a Dragoon revolver.

'This is the Rio Kid's Mexican pard, right enough!' Condon grunted, staring down at the unconscious wagoneer. 'Fiske was right, risin' to the bait and lettin' this feller drive that blastin' powder out of Stateline, just like he didn't suspect nothin' out of the ordinary.'

Jeb O'Malley stooped to hoist Celestino's inert form over his massive shoulder.

'Fiske always plays it close,' O'Malley grunted, as they headed toward the river. 'He didn't dast let one of his own drivers take this freight north tonight. Wouldn't look right if Cap'n Jack choused the load and didn't scalp the driver.'

O'Malley waded out into the icy waters of Lost River, with Condon splashing at his side. At midstream the current was hip deep, but the water shallowed off as they reached the south bank. O'Malley lowered Celestino to the ground.

As if by prearranged plan, three riders emerged from the timber to meet the men in buckskin. The starlight revealed them as Dorian Fiske, the Modoc sub-chieftain Schonchin, and the Lion of the Lavabeds himself, Captain Jack.

'Heap good!' grunted the Modoc chief, speaking in pidgin English for the benefit of the self-styled 'trappers.' 'This is the Mexican who rides with the Rio Kid. I take um back to Lavabeds tonight.'

*   *   *

Captain Jack squatted down to run his scarred hand over Mireles' thick black hair.

'You've never had a Mexican's scalp in yore collection, eh, Kintupash?' chuckled Dorian Fiske, speaking in the Modoc tongue. 'Make shore yuh lift his hair before yuh roast him alive.'

Captain Jack stood up, peering across the river to where the canvas hood of the Conestoga glowed faintly in the dancing rays of the campfire.

'You haul up powder to Lavabeds before dawn?' Captain Jack inquired, turning to Condon and O'Malley.

The men glanced at Fiske, who launched

into an unintelligible discourse with the Modoc chief. When they had finished, Fiske turned to his men.

'The Indians will be waitin' for the wagon at the North Pass tomorrow,' Fiske explained. 'Captain Jack has given me a password for yuh to give when the sentinels challenge yuh. He can't take any chances of a slip-up, with what he has at stake.'

The two 'trappers' nodded, waiting for Fiske to go on.

'The password is *"miculick,"*' Fiske said 'Got it? *Miculick.* That's Modoc lingo for "We come as friends." Yuh're to drive the blastin' powder up a canyon straight to Captain Jack's headquarters, and help the Indians set the fuses and plant the charges along the rimrocks of Flintridge Canyon. Savvy?'

O'Malley grinned. 'Leave it to us, boss,' he said.

Fiske shook hands with the Indians, who proceeded to lift Celestino Mireles' limp form aboard one of the horses. In minutes the Indians had vanished into the trees.

Fiske shuddered. 'I'd hate to be in that Mexican's shoes,' he muttered. 'But I reckon the Rio Kid put him up to it. Come on, men. Let's get that team hitched up.'

CHAPTER ELEVEN

DEATH ON LOST RIVER

Fiske mounted his sorrel gelding and rode down the slope toward the river ford, following his two henchmen who waded out into the river. The gun boss of Stateline was in rare good spirits tonight. No one in the settlement would cast a suspicious eye in his direction when the word got around that another of the Bon Marche's freight wagons had been seized by hostile Modocs en route to Jacksonville.

Several days would elapse before the news got to Stateville that the wagon had mysteriously vanished on its way to the Oregon settlement. Major Tracy Williard would have no cause to connect the robbery of ten barrels of blasting powder with the surprise attack which the Army was scheduling for tomorrow night.

As masterful as Robert Pryor's scheme had been to strike in force at the very nerve center of Captain Jack's defenses in the hitherto impenetrable Lavabeds, Fiske knew that the wily Lion of the Lavabeds would arrange an even more clever rebuttal for the harassed Army.

With the walls of Flintridge Canyon mined with explosive charges, the invading infantrymen would never know what happened to them tomorrow night, let alone having any survivors to bring back a report on what had caused the wholesale slaughter.

Dorian Fiske was whistling a tune as his gelding splashed up on the north bank and headed toward his Conestoga, silhouetted against the dancing flames of the campfire built at the edge of the timber.

The possibility that danger waited at the prairie schooner did not occur to the Stateline outlaw boss. O'Malley and Condon had encountered no difficulty in halting the young Mexican, with their fabricated story of an avalanche blocking the Jacksonville road up ahead.

All that remained to do now was hitch up the team and see the two buckskin-clad men on their way toward the Lavabeds with the blasting powder. Then Fiske would return to the Golden Poppy Saloon without anyone in Stateline having been aware of his absence.

Fiske's horse was flanked by his two henchmen as they approached the grazing team. O'Malley and Condon picked up the lead ropes and started for the wagon, leading three horses each.

They were halting alongside the harness which Celestino Mireles had piled beside the wagon tongue when a calm voice challenged them from the interior of the covered wagon:

'Get your hands up, gentlemen! You're

covered.'

Fiske stiffened in saddle, jerking his head around to stare in the direction of the voice. The first thing he saw was star glow shining on the leveled barrel of an Army carbine, held by a lean, blue-coated figure framed in the oval opening of the Conestoga's hood.

Protruding through the opening were the muzzles of three other rifles.

'Walker Henry!' gasped Fiske, groping his arms skyward. 'What in thunderation—'

The cavalry sergeant climbed out on the wagon seat.

'Fiske!' he said, lowering his gun. 'I didn't— What became of Celestino Mireles? He went out to water the team and didn't come back. What happened to him?'

A furtive grin relaxed Dorian Fiske's evil countenance. In the darkness, then, Sergeant Henry had not witnessed the Mexican's capture or transfer across the river.

'I decided to ride out and overtake my wagon, Sarge,' Fiske explained, lowering his arms. 'This freight is valuable and I didn't know the Mexican from Adam. I jumped at the chance to hire the first driver who volunteered. But on thinking it over, I—'

*   *   *

It was Jeb O'Malley who interrupted Fiske's plot to ward off Henry's suspicions. Thinking

96

that the sergeant was off guard, O'Malley snaked a Dragoon .44 from holster and brought it up, spitting flame.

The trapper's hasty shot plucked a hole in the canvas hood of the wagon. Instantly, the night resounded to a point-blank hail of shots as Henry's troopers opened fire from inside the wagon.

A bullet whipped the beaver hat from Fiske's head. O'Malley went down, drilled between the eyes. Curt Condon, following his partner's lead, had a six-gun blazing in his fist.

With a wild yell, Fiske wheeled his horse to trample O'Malley's corpse and spurred toward the river in getaway, followed by Walker Henry's fast-triggered carbine. Bullets droned past Fiske's ears, but in the dim light the fleeing outlaw made an elusive target. He reached the near bank of Lost River unscathed and sent his gelding hurtling into the water.

Terror clawed at Fiske's vitals as he sent the horse slanting across the white water. Celestino or the Rio Kid had planted an ace in the hole, hiding an escort of troopers in the northbound wagon!

Fiske chewed out an oath as his horse veered off the ford and plunged into swimming water. He gave the gelding its head, clinging to the saddlehorn and cantle rim to keep from being unhorsed by the surging waters.

He knew his outlaw reign in Stateline was finished by tonight's fiasco. Sergeant Henry's testimony would link him with the Modocs, even though actual proof was lacking. Worse yet, the failure to deliver the barrels of blasting powder to Captain Jack and his waiting redskins in the Lavabeds put his Indian friends in dire peril.

The gelding's hoofs got purchase in the shelving mud and waded ashore on the south bank. Across the river, cavalry guns were shooting ineffectually in his direction, the slugs going wild. Fiske reined his pony up to the Stateline road and headed south.

Then, at the edge of the timber, new disaster loomed. Three riders emerged suddenly in front of him, galloping toward Lost River, completely blocking the road. In the dim light, Fiske recognized the trio as he halted his gelding.

The central rider was the Rio Kid. He was accompanied by the Indian girl, Winema, and Frank Riddle.

'Fiske!' Pryor shouted, recognizing the bedraggled figure on the mud-spattered gelding. 'What's goin' on?'

The gun boss of Stateline went berserk, then. He whipped a Colt from holster and notched his gunsights on the Rio Kid's husky frame, squeezing trigger at point-blank range.

But immersion in the icy waters of the Lost River had jammed the gun's mechanism. Before Dorian Fiske could twirl the locked cylinder with his hands, the Rio Kid's .45s were blazing.

A bullet caught Fiske in the chest, jolting him back in saddle. A second slug drilled his cheekbone and ripped out through the base of his skull, terminating the outlaw's violent career in a swirl of gunsmoke.

With a gagging sigh, Fiske slid limply from stirrups. His gelding, panicked by the lead streaking past its muzzle, stampeded down the road past Frank Riddle's horse and was lost to view in the timber.

The Rio Kid swung out of stirrups, pouching his smoking sixes as he knelt to examine Fiske's body. Then he came to his feet, cocking an ear to the shouting across the river.

'Celestino!' Pryor yelled, cupping hands to his mouth. 'It's me, *companero!* Don't shoot. We're coming across!'

Sergeant Walker Henry and three of his troopers were waiting on the north bank when the Rio Kid and his trailmates splashed across the ford.

'Celestino's disappeared, sir!' the sergeant panted, grounding the butt of his rifle.

*   *   *

Pryor felt his veins jelling as he listened to Henry's account of the two Rogue River trappers halting the wagon at the edge of the forest, and Celestino's subsequent disappearance.

'I figger the trappers must have trailed him down to the river and knifed him, Captain!' Henry concluded. 'I've got two of my men scouting the river bank in search of his body. But they might have tossed him into the river. I—I'm afraid we failed you and Celestino tonight, sir.'

Bob Pryor shook his head grimly. Two cavalrymen approached in the darkness to report that they had found no trace of the young Mexican, dead or alive.

A shout from one of the soldiers at the wagon came ringing through the night above the rush of Lost River.

'One of these trappers is still alive, Sarge! He claims Celestino was carried off by the Modocs!'

The Rio Kid spurred into a gallop, skidding Saber to a halt when he reached the Conestoga. His swift glance photographed a tableau as he stepped out of stirrups. Two soldiers were holding the team while another, wearing a corporal's chevrons, was kneeling beside the groaning figure of Curt Condon. A few feet away, Jeb O'Malley lay rigid in death.

Condon was propped up against the hickory wagon tongue. It was obvious that he was mortally wounded and sinking fast. Blood leaked from bullet wounds in his chest and abdomen, but his eyes were open and he appeared to know who the Rio Kid was.

'What did yuh say happened to Celestino?' Pryor demanded, a note of raw fury cracking in his voice.

A gagging cough brought crimson bubbles to Condon's mouth. He wiped off his beard with a buckskin sleeve and his panting whisper was barely audible to Pryor.

'Cap'n Jack an' Schonchin—are on their way to the Lavabeds—with your pard,' Condon whispered. 'Cap'n Jack—knew he—was a spy workin' for Army.'

Pryor felt his backbone turn to an ice pole. Celestino a prisoner of the Modocs was far worse news than if he had learned that his loyal and courageous companion from the Rio Grande had been killed outright.

* * *

Winema and her husband rode up and dismounted in time to hear Condon resume his confession.

'My sand is runnin' out fast,' the outlaw wheezed. 'I'll try—make up for—my part in this—business. Never did cotton to workin' for redskins—but Dorian Fiske—our boss—he was quarterblood Modoc—hisself.'

The Rio Kid bent an ear to catch the dying man's whisper.

'Fiske wanted blastin' powder—to reach Cap'n Jack. O'Malley an' me to haul it—through North Pass—deliver it to Modocs.

Cap'n Jack—give Fiske password—to get us through Injun lines. *Miculick*—password.'

Condon's voice trailed off in a paroxysm of coughing which left him spent and ashen, hardly breathing. The Rio Kid stirred restlessly, impatient with the irrelevant turn Condon's talk had taken.

Fiske's plans, the mumbojumbo of Modoc passwords, these were not the things that he wanted to hear from Condon's lips.

'Listen to me, fella,' the Rio Kid said anxiously. 'I want to know if Dorian Fiske is the man who has been supplyin' the Modocs with smuggled goods all along? I've got to know for shore. Fiske is dead, fella. Nod yore head if you can't talk.'

Condon settled back against the wagon tongue, fighting for breath.

'Fiske—wasn't—man you want,' was the dying man's surprising statement. 'Fiske was just go-between—for Cap'n Jack's real tillicum. The man—you want—'

Condon's head sagged on his chest and his whisper trailed off into nothingness, choked by a gurgling rattle in his windpipe.

The Rio Kid reached out to feel for a pulse in Condon's wrist, convinced that the man was dead. But he felt a faint throb of life still moving through the artery.

'He's lapsed into a coma,' Pryor said, standing up. 'Winema, will you stand by in case he comes to? It seems Dorian Fiske ain't the renegade Major Williard is after!'

CHAPTER TWELVE

DESPERATE PLAN

Loosening the rawhide thongs which laced the unconscious trapper's buckskin jacket to ease the man's breathing, the Indian girl took her place at his side.

The Rio Kid moved off into the darkness, feeling the need to be alone, to wrestle with the overpowering grief which the news of Celestino's fate had brought home to him.

He turned over in his mind the statement which the dying trapper had made regarding Fiske's villainy. And suddenly, out of the chaos of tragedy which bogged his thinking, the Rio Kid conceived an idea.

He called to Frank Riddle, saw the interpreter detach himself from the silent group of soldiers and walk over to him.

'Frank, yuh've risked yore life a good many times since the Modoc War began,' the Rio Kid said. 'I'm about to ask yuh to side me in a scheme which mebbe will cost both of us our lives. But it should go a long ways towards windin' up the Modoc War and bringin' peace back to this country.'

Winema's husband nodded soberly. 'I am at

your service, Captain,' the interpreter said.

The Rio Kid drew in a deep breath.

'Captain Jack is expectin' this wagon to show up at the north end of the Lavabeds,' he said. 'Two of Fiske's men are supposed to be aboard that wagon. Yuh heard Fiske's man mention the password which would put 'em through the Indian sentry lines?'

Riddle nodded. '"*Miculick*,"' he said. 'That's Modoc patois for "We come as friends."'

The Rio Kid rubbed his stubbly jaw thoughtfully, shaping up details of his hazy, still ephemeral plan in his mind before outlining it to Riddle.

'Why can't you and me deliver them barrels of explosives to Captain Jack tomorrow?' he asked. 'We could make out we were Fiske's men. You could shave off that beard and change clothes with the dead man yonder. I doubt if the Modocs would recognize yuh as Winema's husband. And none of the Indians know me.'

Riddle eyed the Rio Kid sharply.

'I am willing to do anything to help the cause,' he said, 'but why play into the Indians' hands by delivering that blasting powder, when you know it will be used to destroy hundreds of Major Williard's men tomorrow night?'

The Rio Kid smiled bleakly and reached out to lay a hand on the interpreter's shoulder.

'We'll deliver a wagon load of barrels to

the Lavabeds, Frank,' he explained, 'but the barrels won't have no blasting powder in 'em. We'll load 'em with plain sand.'

The doubt left Riddle's face then. He turned to peer through the darkness to where his Indian wife maintained her vigil beside Curt Condon's unconscious form.

'Winema will have to accompany us, Captain,' he said. 'She is the only person outside the Lavabeds who knows the lay of the land. She will guide us through North Pass.'

The Rio Kid hesitated, momentarily deciding to call off the whole scheme rather than involve a woman in such a dangerous undertaking. Then he realized that Winema had dedicated herself to bringing the bloody Modoc conflict to a stop, on behalf of her tribesmen who gave a cruel and sadistic chief their blind and unthinking obedience.

'Good,' Pryor said, grinning with relief. 'Keep our plans to yoreself, Frank. I'm believin' Sergeant Henry and his men are reliable, but we'll take no chances.'

As they rejoined the silent group by the wagon, Winema looked up from her place beside the prostrate Condon.

'He is dead, sir,' the Indian girl reported. The Rio Kid accepted the news philosophically. Condon had carried into eternity the secret of who had been the guiding hand back of Dorian Fiske's smuggling activities with the Indians.

'Sergeant,' Pryor said, turning to Walker Henry, 'detail a couple of yore men to dig graves for these renegades. Yuh'll find shovels lashed to the wagon box yonder.'

* * *

While the troopers were engaged in shoveling out two graves, the Rio Kid unbuckled his saddlebags from Saber's kak.

'That'll do, men,' Pryor said, as the soldiers prepared to lift the dead men into the excavations. 'We'll finish the burial, Riddle and me. Sergeant, I want you to head back to Major Williard's right off. Take our three horses. We'll ride the wagon back to town.'

'Yes sir,' Sergeant Henry responded, saluting.

'Tell Major Williard that there haven't been no changes in our main plan, Sergeant,' the Rio Kid went on. 'Yuh can tell him that I'll take the responsibility for the Riddles' safety, if he asks yuh about quittin' yore post in Stateline.'

Two corporals mounted the Riddles' horses while the privates shouldered their rifles and fell into squad formation. Winema stared inquiringly at Pryor but said nothing. She knew from the gravity on her husband's face that something was up.

The soldiers marched briskly toward the river, Sergeant Henry in their lead mounted on Saber. That was a concession on the dun's part, as if he understood the gravity of the situation. For it was a rare thing that Saber even let a stranger come near.

From his saddlebags the Rio Kid removed a leather case containing soap and razor, which he handed to Riddle.

'Shave off them whiskers, Frank,' he ordered the interpreter. 'Yuh'll likely find hot water over at the trappers' camp yonder. Yuh can tell Winema what's up while yuh're shavin'.'

When the Riddles had departed in the direction of the dying campfire, Pryor busied himself removing the buckskin jackets and mountaineer boots from the two dead men. Then he finished burying Fiske's henchmen and went on to the job of hitching the six Morgans to the Conestoga.

That done, Pryor mounted the wagon and drove down to the edge of Lost River. He unsnapped the end gate of the mudwagon and rolled the heavy powder barrels off onto the ground one by one.

He had removed the wooden plugs from the bungholes of the barrels and was emptying the heavy black grains of blasting powder from the first barrel into the river when Frank Riddle and Winema rejoined him. Glancing at Riddle, Pryor grinned. Without his heavy sideburns and long beard, the interpreter looked like a different man, his face appearing sharp and narrow.

'I feel like a plucked goose,' Riddle chuckled, stroking his white cheeks. 'I hope I will appear like one to the Modocs.'

Winema and her husband fell to work emptying the gunpowder barrels into the river. When they were at work on the last barrel, Pryor poured a sizable mound of powder out on the ground, for future use.

Refilling the barrels with riverbank sand was the next job. Winema, with typical Indian ingenuity, fashioned a funnel from a slab of thin bark and held it in position over the bungholes of the barrels while Pryor and her husband shoveled coarse sand into the casks.

The pale promise of dawn was staining the eastern horizon by the time they had loaded the barrels, filling the area under the bunghole openings with real gunpowder. Then, hammering the wooden stoppers back into place, the two men rigged two poles from the ground to the wagon bed to serve as a ramp and rolled the sand-laden barrels into the Conestoga, using a rope parbuckle.

'We won't reach the entrance to North Pass by daylight, as Fiske's men would have done,' Pryor said, climbing into the driver's seat. He had already deposited there the clothing he had removed from Condon and O'Malley. 'When the Modocs halt us at the edge of the Lavabeds I'll tell 'em in sign language that we broke a wheel and had to stop and fix it up.'

Winema, whose presence on the trek was imperative for guide purposes, concealed herself under an Army blanket among the powder barrels. Her husband joined the Rio Kid on the driver's seat and they started their perilous journey. Soon they had forded the river and were heading south-eastward toward the blazing sunrise and the Lavabeds . . .

*   *   *

The California sun was nooning by the time Winema had directed the plodding team into the northern outskirts of the Lavabeds. Realizing that they were under surveillance of hidden Modoc sentries, the Rio Kid and Frank Riddle had donned the heavy fringed hunting coats they had taken from Fiske's slain partners.

Winema, keeping out of sight inside the hooded Conestoga, gave Pryor directions which enabled him to choose the vast lava-walled chasm which was North Pass. Without the Indian girl's expert guidance, they could easily have driven the wagon into any one of a hundred blind cul-de-sacs where it would have been impossible to turn around and retrace their route.

'I thought Williard's troops kept a cordon around the entire Lavabeds,' Pryor remarked moodily as he tooled the lurching wagon up a long grade. 'I don't see how we come this far without sightin' an American patrol.'

The Rio Kid broke off as the lead horses snorted in alarm and came to a halt. Out of a fissure in the North Pass wall stepped two big Modoc warriors, clad only in breech clouts and moccasins and carrying American Army rifles.

In response to their guttural challenge, the Rio Kid stood up in the wagon box, grinned broadly, lifted an arm in the sign of peace and called loudly:

'*Miculick.*'

The password which Captain Jack had given Dorian Fiske had a magic reaction on the two braves. Their hostile visages relaxed and they began an excited discourse in their native tongue, gesticulating and pointing toward the east.

'I'm not supposed to savvy Modoc—which I don't!' the Rio Kid muttered from the corner of his mouth. 'What are they sayin', Frank?'

Riddle grinned bleakly.

'They say we were expected at dawn, but that we can proceed to the Fountain of the Gods without worrying about the American troops. It seems that Schonchin and his warriors started a battle east of here at dawn and drew Williard's guards away from North Pass.'

CHAPTER THIRTEEN

PASSWORD TO PERIL

Cracking his long whip over the leaders, the Rio Kid sent the weary Morgans lunging into their traces. The Modoc sentries stepped aside as the wagon rumbled past their lookout post and headed up the grade.

Wheel tracks were visible on the scarred lava, indicating that other wagons had been to the Lavabeds before the occupants of the Conestoga. The grade leveled off and they began a tortuous route, following the ridge of a twisting plateau, which led toward the heart of the *pedregal.*

Once, passing the mouth of a side gulch, their ears caught the far-off sound of sporadic gunfire. That would be Schonchin and his warriors, engaging the American soldiery in a deceptive action to clear North Pass for the transit of their wagon.

The sun was westering in their eyes when the Rio Kid recognized a pinnacle of rock. It was, he knew, a landmark near the site of Captain Jack's headquarters at the mouth of Flintridge Canyon.

He halted the blowing team and poked his head inside the Conestoga, smiling at Winema huddled back among the sand-filled powder barrels.

'I can make it on to Captain Jack's headquarters from here, Winema,' he said. 'You can hide yoreself till we get back with the wagon. It wouldn't do for the Modocs to catch yuh. It would give the whole trick away.'

Tears misted Frank Riddle's eyes as he helped the pretty squaw out of the wagon. He embraced her tenderly and they whispered together for a few moments, man and wife taking leave of each other for what might well be the last time.

Riddle's clean-shaven face showed no sign of emotion when he climbed back aboard the wagon. Winema had slipped off into the tangled lava formations to await their return.

The Rio Kid whipped the team into motion, conscious of a dull, throbbing ache of suspense knotting his stomach. They were nearing the den of the Lion of the Lavabeds now, would soon be running the gauntlet of Modoc eyes.

Captain Jack was expecting two of Dorian Fiske's wagoneers to deliver this blasting cargo to his stronghold. What if he knew Condon and O'Malley personally? But the Rio Kid had weighed that possibility before embarking on this mission, and was resigned to the gamble.

A quarter of a mile from the demolished Great Cave, Indian lookouts caught sight of the plodding prairie schooner approaching through the Lavabeds and heralded its approach with exultant whoops. By the time the wagon drew in sight of the Fountain of the Gods, the Rio Kid and Frank Riddle saw that the majority of Captain Jack's fighting men were awaiting their arrival.

Pryor's face gave no hint of the inner strain he was under as he halted the team on the open ground between the ruined cavern and the artesian well. Hundreds of Indians thronged around the Conestoga, lifting the canvas flaps to peer at the barrels which the wagon contained.

Then an aisle formed in the milling mass of red-skinned warriors and the Rio Kid found himself face to face with the Lion of the Lavabeds himself.

Captain Jack lifted a hand in greeting, his coal-black eyes shuttling between the Rio Kid and Frank Riddle. The interpreter had prudently climbed back into the wagon, knowing that his wife's cousin might recognize him without his beard.

'How,' Captain Jack greeted the wagon driver. 'You come heap late. Fiske promise wagon get here after dawn.'

The Rio Kid wrapped his lines around the Jacob's staff and clambered down the front wheel to stand within arm's reach of the Lion of the Lavabeds.

*   *   *

A nonchalant grin was on Pryor's dust-grimed

113

face. Captain Jack had shown no suspicious sign upon their arrival, patent evidence that he did not know the men Dorian Fiske had assigned to bring the wagon into the Lavabeds. And he had never seen the Rio Kid before. As long as Frank Riddle kept out of sight inside the wagon, all would be well.

'Have um heap trouble with wheel,' Pryor alibied, indicating with elaborate pantomime that the front wheel of the mudwagon had come off the axle en route, forcing a delay while they made repairs. 'We unload powder, get um back to Stateline, huh?'

Captain Jack's dour face eyed the Rio Kid inscrutably.

'Injun no savvy blasting powder,' he said. 'Fiske say you help um Modocs fix um powder along Flintridge Canyon.'

The Rio Kid nodded.

'We fix um,' he said, and clambered back into the wagon, intending to drive his heavy load of barrels closer to Flintridge Canyon before unloading.

In the act of unwrapping his lines, the Rio Kid paused. Staring off across the heads of the assembled Modocs, he caught sight of a lone figure lashed to a wooden post out in front of the avalanche debris which blocked the mouth of the Great Cave.

It was Celestino Mireles, awaiting torture by fire. Even as the Rio Kid stared, he saw his loyal Mexican comrade flash him a swift grin of recognition.

The Rio Kid tore his gaze from Celestino and turned to release his hand brake. He saw Captain Jack staring at him quizzically, and he jerked a thumb in the direction of the torture stake.

'Fix um to fry Mexican boy, huh?' he asked, with a forced chuckle.

Captain Jack rubbed his war-painted cheek with a knuckle. 'Are you same paleface who captured him last night?' the Lion of the Lavabeds demanded.

The Rio Kid nodded, letting a hand slide in the direction of the Colt strapped to his right thigh. He was not aware that Captain Jack had seen Celestino's captors the night before.

Now, if ever, was the high moment of their danger. If he saw the slightest hint of suspicion in the Modoc chieftain's attitude, he intended to fire at least one shot before Captain Jack gave the signal to seize him. And that one bullet would down the leader of the Modocs!

'Shore,' he said grinning. 'Mexican boy yonder drive um wagon from Stateline to my camp on Lost River last night.'

Captain Jack nodded, leaning on his grounded rifle. 'Mexican boy burns tonight,' the Modoc answered. 'After blasting powder send paleface soldiers to happy hunting grounds.'

Whipsawing his lines, the Rio Kid started his wagon, skirting the artesian well. His exhausted team, famished for water, broke into a trot as Pryor steered in the direction of Flintridge Canyon.

Out of range of Captain Jack's vision, the Rio Kid breathed easier. The crisis was past. The Modocs had accepted them as trusted whites, colleagues of Dorian Fiske. Frank Riddle had succeeded in keeping out of sight of the one Indian most likely to see through his smooth-shaven disguise—Captain Jack.

Spending the rest of the day assisting the Indians in setting the 'powder' charges at strategic points along the rimrocks of Flintridge Canyon was exactly in line with the Rio Kid's desires. It meant he could stay in the vicinity of Captain Jack's stronghold, close enough to make an attempt to save Celestino Mireles' life if an opportunity presented itself. It must—or he would make one.

A dense fog was beginning to gather over the Lavabeds, a natural phenomenon which had harassed Major Tracy Williard's offensive tactics in the past, adding to the cover which the Modocs enjoyed inside the Lavabeds. Tonight, however, the fog would be doubly useful in masking the overwater approach of Williard's raft-borne troops.

*   *   *

The poor visibility might present difficulties in landing the rafts at the Devil's Eye. But unless

116

a wind sprung up to roughen the waters of Tule Lake, Pryor had every reason to believe that the Army's part in the operation would be carried off successfully.

Two score of husky copper-skinned Modoc warriors followed the wagon to a point immediately in front of the canyon which was to be Williard's route of approach to the Fountain of the Gods this coming midnight. The Rio Kid halted his wagon, set the brakes and swung to the ground, followed by Frank Riddle.

'Anybody here speak um English?' Pryor asked. He knew it would be imprudent to converse through the medium of Frank Riddle. White men conversant with the Modoc tongue were rare, and Riddle was known to be one of the few interpreters outside the Modoc tribe.

'Me spik um heap good,' announced a grinning young warrior in his late teens. 'We help um carry round boxes.'

The Rio Kid unchained the tail-gate and directed the Indians to unload the powder barrels. Riddle climbed into the wagon and emerged with a box of fuses and pliers for cutting the detonating devices into proper lengths.

The remaining hours of the afternoon were busy ones for Riddle and Bob Pryor and their Indian porters. At regularly-spaced intervals along the canyon walls, they buried barrels which the Indians, jabbering among themselves, spoke of as 'thunder boxes.' To each barrel, the Rio Kid affixed a fuse.

Around dusk, when the last barrel of river sand had been placed where, had it been explosive, its detonation would have crumbled the decomposing lava walls into the canyon, the Rio Kid summoned the Indian helpers about him for a demonstration.

Opening the last barrel, Pryor poured out a cupful portion of black powder from the small amount of explosive which he had used to mask the contents of the sand-filled barrels. Pouring the heavy black kernels of powder on a flat rock, Pryor fixed a length of fuse thereto, took out flint and steel and lighted the end.

The Indians chattered excitedly as they saw the wormlike length of fuse spit off a stream of sparks, fuming white smoke as its core burned toward the small heap of powder. The black stuff ignited with a blinding flare and sent a great mushroom of white smoke puffing off into the fog-heavy atmosphere.

Used to nothing more powerful than gunpowder, the Modocs fell back in momentary panic at the surprising volume of the explosion caused by so small an amount of powder. Then, reassembling a few yards away, they talked excitedly among themselves.

'They're going back to report on the white man's thunder to Captain Jack,' Frank Riddle interpreted their jabberings for the Rio Kid's benefit. 'Your demonstration was a big success, Captain.'

Preceded by their Indian helpers, the Rio Kid and Frank Riddle started back toward Captain Jack's stronghold, following the twisting rim of the Flintridge gorge. So far as the Indians were concerned, all was in readiness for tonight's secret raid by Major Williard's forces.

According to conversation which Riddle had overheard among the Indians during the afternoon, Captain Jack would assign a warrior to each powder barrel. When the American soldiers were strung out in full force in the canyon below, the Modoc war drums would beat a signal. Each warrior would light his fuse and then flee for safety. In a matter of moments, the white man's 'thunderbolts' would blast the walls of Flintridge Canyon into the chasm, crushing the white soldiers under thousands of tons of plummeting lava!

Then, to celebrate their victory over the white enemy, Captain Jack and his *Maklak* tribesmen would launch a celebration with firewater and victory dances, culminating with the torture of their white captive, Celestino Mireles.

'I'll have to report to Captain Jack when we get back,' the Rio Kid said. 'You get into the wagon, Frank, where yuh won't be seen at too close range. I reckon we're to head back toward Stateline now that our powder-plantin'

119

job is finished.'

Returning to the head of the canyon, Frank Riddle climbed into the waiting wagon while the Rio Kid followed their Indian porters into camp.

CHAPTER FOURTEEN

WHITE TRAITOR

Glowing torchlight fires illumined the open area in front of the Great Cave, and it appeared to Bob Pryor that the Lavabeds were aswarm with Modocs. On the outskirts of the war camp squaws had pitched their teepees. Obviously, Captain. Jack had summoned his entire tribe to witness the final crushing overthrow of the invading whites. Indians of all ages, from papooses to white-haired oldsters too infirm for active fighting duty, had assembled at the Fountain of the Gods to witness the blasting of Flintridge Canyon and the celebration to follow.

'Major Williard's goin' to have a battle on his hands,' the Rio Kid thought soberly as he headed toward a central bonfire built near the artesian well, where the tribal chieftains were congregated. 'But when that blastin' powder fails to explode, the Major at least will have the advantage of surprise.'

The Rio Kid halted just outside the range of firelight where the chiefs were gathered in pow-wow. He hoped against hope that Captain Jack would not insist on his facing the other chiefs, for the presence of Boston Charley and Hooker Jim in their midst would be fatal. The two chieftains would be sure to recognize him as the white man they had planned to torture in the cabin above Stateline a week ago.

Pryor breathed easier when he saw the Lion of the Lavabeds move out of the council circle and walk toward him, accompanied by the Indians who had spent the afternoon planting barrels of supposed blasting powder along the canyon walls.

Captain Jack's cruel visage was wreathed in smiles as he held a hand out to the Rio Kid.

'Heap good, paleface friend!' the Modoc leader grunted. 'You go now to Fiske. Tell um Injun have big victory tonight. Tell um Fiske he get heap big pay for help.'

The Rio Kid bowed. A single question now might solve the enigma which Curt Condon had carried with him in death—the name of the renegade for whom Dorian Fiske, the gun boss of Stateline, was a mere underling. But the Rio Kid dared not voice that question. Every moment he remained in Captain Jack's camp was at the risk of exposure—and torture to follow. Obviously, his mission as wagoneer and powder-setter was over, and Captain Jack was dismissing him.

'I go,' Pryor grunted, lifting his arm in the tribal salute. 'Me tell um Fiske what you say. Heap big massacre tonight, huh?'

Captain Jack turned on his heel and stalked back to rejoin his chiefs. From the corner of his eye, Pryor saw a number of fat Modoc squaws waddling out to meet Frank Riddle in the wagon, carrying baskets of food for their white benefactors.

On the pretense of threading his way through the throngs of Modocs massed between the hemming lava walls, the Rio Kid pushed his way toward the torture stake where Celestino Mireles was being held prisoner. In the clotted shadows, he aroused no attention as he approached his Mexican friend.

His throat constricted as he saw that a great heap of brush and dry tules, hauled up from the shore of the Lake, had been piled as high as Celestino's waist. Fuel for the torture fires which Captain Jack would kindle personally if the Modocs' plan for a victory celebration materialized!

A group of chattering Indian children, borrowing the sadistic traits of their elders, were dancing in serpentine around the torture stake where Celestino stood, pelting the helpless Mexican with willow switches and small pebbles of lava.

Celestino looked gaunt and wretched as the Rio Kid approached. Pryor's angry cry silenced the dancing children, who withdrew in awe of the white man.

'You weel help me, General?' moaned Celestino, his dusky face a mass of bruises where hard-flung pebbles had lacerated his cheeks.

*   *   *

A vast pity welled up in the Rio Kid as he gazed at his Mexican friend. His hand closed over the hilt of his bowie knife, and he fought back a wild impulse to slash Celestino's bonds and make an attempt to shoot his way to freedom, back to back.

'Yuh're not scheduled to be burned till after the Major's troops are buried alive in the canyon tonight, Celestino,' he whispered rapidly. 'I haven't got time to explain now, but that won't happen. By midnight, Major Williard's troops will be wipin' out these savages.'

Celestino grinned through puffed and bleeding lips.

'*Esta bueno*,' he whispered dully.

'I'm here with Frank Riddle and Winema,' the Rio Kid went on. 'We're supposed to drive the wagon out of the Lavabeds, but don't worry, *amigo*. We'll be around close. I'll show up when the fun starts tonight.'

A big Modoc buck, carrying a pistol in either hand, moved toward the torture stake as he recognized the identity of Celestino's visitor. With a parting word of assurance for his friend, the Rio Kid walked over to the guard.

'Heap big fire tonight, huh?' Pryor grinned.

The Indian shrugged, his dark face immobile. Leaving him, Pryor soon was elbowing his way through the squaws massed around the waiting Conestoga. He climbed into the wagon, finding the seat stacked high with baskets and pottery dishes filled with Indian food.

'Let's go, Frank!' Pryor muttered, with a final backward glance at the Indian assemblage. 'We'll drive the wagon back into the Lavabeds a ways and pick up Winema. Then I aim to double back and be ready to help Celestino when the ruckus breaks loose at midnight.'

*　　　*　　　*

Miles Elkorn's sawmill camp was a beehive of activity as a rolling inshore fog brought premature darkness to the California timber country. Working day and night for the past three days, Elkorn's crews of buckers and fallers had hewn trees in the neighboring forest and snaked the big logs by means of ox teams to the waiting sawmill.

There, the logs had been converted into whipsawed planks and heavy dimension lumber. Shifts of carpenters had fashioned the massive timbers into vast rafts, working under cover of Elkorn's stockade to prevent their activity being seen by hostile spies.

Now, with darkness settling over the land, the tension deepened as Miles Elkorn took personal command of dragging the big rafts down to the edge of Tule Lake and launching them.

Under cover of the night, Major Tracy Williard marched into the sawmill camp with three companies of picked infantrymen, each man carrying sixty rounds of ammunition and cooked rations for two days. The army commander and Miles Elkorn conversed briefly by the lake shore as the troops stood at ease in platoon formation.

Out in the shallow water where the rafts floated side by side, workboats were drawn up with twenty of Elkorn's burly lumberjacks in each boat, their oars ready to supply the motive power to tow the loaded rafts across the intervening body of water to the rim of the Lavabeds.

'The rafts are ready—the boatmen are ready,' Miles Elkorn reported. 'I couldn't build a dock out into the lake for fear of tippin' off the Indian scouts on the far shore that somethin' was up. Everything has been done under strict secrecy restrictions, Major.'

The veteran infantry commander grinned in the foggy darkness. 'Thank God for the help of a citizen of your patriotism, Elkorn,' he said fervently. 'How about this fog? This Devil's Eye may be tricky to locate.'

Miles Elkorn shook his head. 'I'll go with yuh across, Major,' he volunteered. 'I know Tule Lake like the palm of my hand, fog or sunshine.'

*　　*　　*

During the next hour, the troops, maintaining strict silence and under orders not to light cigarettes or pipes, marched squad by squad down to the water's edge where Elkorn assigned them to rafts, a hundred men to each raft.

When five of the rafts were loaded with personnel, the sixth was stocked with ammunition and provisions by quartermaster privates from the Rogue River supply base eighty miles north. By ten o'clock, Major Williard and Miles Elkorn waded out to board one of the tow boats, and all was in readiness.

Units of the Oregon Mounted Militia, the California Volunteer Rifles and regular Army troopers of the 21st Infantry were aboard the rafts, keyed to a high pitch and grateful for the privilege of being selected to participate in the historic midnight assault on the Lavabeds. For, if the Rio Kid's plans went as scheduled, the Modoc tyrants would be destroyed for all time.

Miles Elkorn called a low order through the

swimming fog. Oarsmen dipped paddle blades into the icy water. Tow hawsers tightened. Heavily-armed troopers braced themselves as the big rafts started moving away from the shore.

Shrouded in cottony fog which hugged the surface of Tule Lake, the rafts moved six abreast across the placid waters. Five hundred troopers closing in on the Lavabeds with the stealth of a cougar stalking its prey!

Unerringly, Miles Elkorn guided the waterborne raiders to the precise point on the eastern shore where the Devil's Eye spilled out the trickle of artesian water from the Modocs' Fountain of the Gods, a mile inland by way of Flintridge Canyon.

Towboats scraped their keels on the submerged shelf of mud which the Devil's Eye stream had built out into the Lake. Troopers adjusted their rifle slings and, at an order from their lieutenants, stepped out into knee-deep water and moved ashore, lining up in battle array.

'From here on it's yore party, Major,' Miles Elkorn said, as he and the Army. commander waded through the shoulder-high tules. 'I'll stay here with my boatmen. Good luck.'

Major Williard reached out to grip the lumber king's hand in the darkness. The landing had been made with ease, and only the trilling of mud frogs broke the fog-shrouded silence.

'Thanks for everything, Elkorn. I'll see that President Grant hears of the part you played in this coup tonight.'

Elkorn's pock-scarred face froze into grim lines as he saw Major Williard move off to confer with his staff officers. In a few minutes, the troopers would enter the Devil's Eye and deploy up the twisting length of Flintridge Canyon.

Elkorn went back to the lake's edge to where his boatmen were congregated.

'Row back to the sawmill, men,' he ordered. 'I'm goin' along to see the fun.'

The loggers grunted assent and saw their employer head off toward the looming cliff.

But Miles Elkorn did not seek out Major Williard. Unseen in the darkness, the California lumber baron scuttled through the looming cavern which was the Devil's Eye and headed up Flintridge Canyon at a run.

A half-hour later, winded by his exertion, Miles Elkorn was climbing out of the canyon mouth to face the roaring beacon fires of Captain Jack's stronghold. Indians stationed along the rimrocks called out greetings to Elkorn as they recognized the towering giant in the red mackinaw and coonskin cap. Then Miles Elkorn was shaking hands with Captain Jack, addressing him in the halting Modoc language which he had picked up.

'All is ready, Kintupash!' Elkorn panted, gesturing toward the canyon. 'The American troops are even now sneakin' up the canyon. Yuh're all set to spring the trap?'

Captain Jack nodded, exposing crooked fangs in a triumphant grin.

'The gods be thanked for your warning us of this trap, my friend,' the Lion of the Lavabeds said. 'The blasting powder is waiting to be set off by my warriors. Not a white soldier will escape alive!'

CHAPTER FIFTEEN

THE STARS AND STRIPES

Night was alive with an electric tension, as the news spread among the Modocs that the white enemy was even at this minute advancing up Flintridge Canyon, seeking to strike a paralyzing blow at the Modoc fastness—but nearing their own doom with every forward step!

Miles Elkorn sauntered over to the torture stake where Celestino Mireles stood helpless in his bonds, waist-deep in tinder-dry fuel which would char him to a crisp before another sunrise.

'Senor Elkorn!' the Mexican gasped, recognizing the smallpox-pitted face leering at him in the firelight.

'Yes, my spy friend!' taunted the sawmill

boss. 'Yuh didn't expect to see me at yore farewell party tonight, eh?'

Celestino could only stare at the white traitor, as comprehension of Elkorn's perfidy slowly penetrated his brain.

'Then—then you are the *maldito* hombre who captured the Rio Keed that night in Stateline!' he accused thickly. 'Eet was you who questioned heem een that leetle *cabana* on the heelside!'

Elkorn nodded, thrusting a briar pipe between his teeth and lighting it, his face like a satan's mask in the match glow.

'Yes. From the first I've passed along Major Williard's secrets to my red friends in the Lavabeds, Celestino. Dorian Fiske and I have a great stake in seein' the Modocs win this war against the whites.'

Mireles shook his head uncomprehendingly. 'But you are a white!' he protested. 'You play the traitor to your own breed!'

Elkorn laughed harshly. 'I can build up an empire of my own,' the traitorous sawyer, explained, 'as long as other whites don't get a chance at this land. With the help of the Indians I can become the most powerful man on the Pacific Coast!'

Elkorn broke off. His ears had caught a remote throb of Modoc tom-toms, coming from the lookouts posted along the rim of Flintridge Canyon.

The signal for Captain Jack's warriors to

130

light the fuses of the powder barrels scattered along the south wall of the canyon! The signal which warned the waiting Modocs that their white enemy was approaching their stronghold!

Along the dark-shrouded rimrocks, a dozen warriors fired their fuses and scuttled to safety in the rocks. But the Modoc gods were angry tonight. Something was wrong. The fuses sizzled their way into the buried barrels—and spewed out harmlessly!

The thumping of war drums wavered off, ceased. The tense, expectant Indians massed around the Fountain of the Gods heard another sound welling from the throat of Flintridge Canyon—the brassy notes of a bugle sounding the charge, its strident blast megaphoned into a trumpet of doom by the sounding-boards of the cliff walls.

And then, out into the glare of firelight, burst a line of blue-coated soldiers behind fixed bayonets, fanning out to block off the Indians' only avenues of retreat from the council ground. In their vanguard came a trooper flanking Major Tracy Williard, bearing the regimental colors of the U.S. Infantry and the glorious banner of the Stars and Stripes!

Captain Robert Pryor, crouched down on a ledge overlooking Captain Jack's camp, leaped to his feet as he saw Major Williard's charging troopers fire a heavy salvo at the dismayed ranks of red-skinned warriors who faced them.

Six-gun palmed, the Rio Kid skidded his way down the steep lava slope, unnoticed by the panic-stricken Modocs who saw their best fighters being decimated by the concentrated fire of American riflemen.

Sprinting past the debris-stoppered mouth of the Great Cave, the buckskin-clad Texan snatched a knife out of its scabbard. As he raced up to the torture stake Celestino Mireles stood shouting encouragement to the American soldiers who poured out of Flintridge Canyon in a never-ending stream.

*　　　*　　　*

A slicing thrust of his knife slashed Celestino's bonds in two, and then the Rio Kid was kicking the kindling wood away from his partner's body to get at the ropes which pinioned his legs.

'Senor Elkorn ees the man you want, General!' Celestino yelled in Pryor's ear, as the Rio Kid thrust one of his Colt .45s into the Mexican's hand. 'He ees here een camp tonight, *si!*'

Indescribable confusion reigned in the Indian stronghold. Warriors, breaking the chains of their paralysis, opened fire on the swarming infantrymen who were boiling in a blue tidal wave out of Flintridge Canyon. But the redskins' counter attack was poorly organized, and they began throwing down their rifles in surrender as they saw their fellow braves being slaughtered like flies.

Miles Elkorn, seeing his dreams of empire going up in gunsmoke and the flash of red-dripping bayonets, sprinted toward a break in the cliffs which would lead him to a dubious sanctuary back in the Lavabeds. But the fleeting traitor to his country's cause found his path blocked by a familiar figure in buckskins, sided by a grinning Mexican in the garb of a Chihuahua *hidalgo.*

The Rio Kid's thumb was poised on gun hammer as he saw the pock-scarred sawmill boss skid to a halt in front of him, horror in his eyes as he realized his escape was cut off.

'Get yore hands up, Elkorn!' the Rio Kid's shout sounded above the roar of pitched battle behind the sawyer. 'I'll see yuh hanged along with Captain Jack and yore other *compadres!*'

With a hoarse oath, Elkorn whipped back the tails of his mackinaw and pawed a six-gun from holster. He swung into a killer's crouch as he opened fire on the spread-legged Army scout before him, saw his bullets knock lava chips from the cliff behind Pryor.

With grim precision, the Rio Kid tripped gun hammer. Through founting gunsmoke he saw Elkorn go down on one knee, fighting for the strength to lift his fuming Colt while his left hand clawed at a blood-spouting bullet-hole in his chest.

'I wasn't—born to hang—Rio Kid!'

Pryor held his fire as he saw the gun slip from Miles Elkorn's nerveless fingers. With a convulsive shudder, the lumber king pitched face down in the dirt, a puddle of crimson spreading under his corpse.

The Rio Kid glanced around to see that Celestino Mireles had left his side. A dozen yards away, he saw the Mexican from the Rio Grande engaged in a slugging match with a tall Indian from whose short-bobbed hair jutted a red-tipped eagle feather.

Captain Jack, deserting his tribe in their hour of doom, had been blocked in getaway by the Mexican he had planned to scalp and burn alive before this fateful night was over!

The Lion of the Lavabeds lashed out frantically with his tomahawk, having no time to pull the six-gun from his baldric. But the war ax failed to strike his elusive target. With powerful lefts and rights, Celestino Mireles was chopping Captain Jack's ugly visage into a bloody ruin of pulped flesh and dented bone.

Not until he had beaten the Modoc tyrant into unconsciousness did Celestino glance around to see that the Rio Kid had witnessed the unthroning of the Modoc war lord.

Order was slowly coming out of the frenzied chaos around them. The last of Major Williard's troops had stormed out of the canyon, eager to do battle but finding only a host of surrendering, thoroughly beaten Indians facing them.

Warriors and their squaws and sobbing children were being marshaled into trembling crowds surrounded by cordons of bayonets. The acrid smell of gunpowder blended with the odor of the Modocs' victory fires. The ground around the Fountain of the Gods was littered with dead and dying, with redskin casualties outnumbering the American invaders fifty to one.

*   *   *

Schonchin, Boston Charley, Hooker Jim and lesser chieftains of Captain Jack's band were already being manacled with 'Oregon Boots' around their legs. Army surgeons moved among the fallen fighters, administering first aid to wounded infantrymen.

Then the bugle trumpeted the cease fire order, and a brooding silence settled over the Lavabeds to symbolize the stirring end of the Modoc campaign.

Frank Riddle and Winema came down from the heights where they had witnessed the climactic struggle, to watch Celestino Mireles dragging Captain Jack over to the spot where Sergeant Walker Henry was questioning Schonchin and the other chiefs.

'This is a sad hour for my people,' Winema said gently, 'but it is also the beginning of their redemption. Without evil leadership such as my cousin Kintupash's they will settle down on their hunting lands and prosper as never before.'

The Rio Kid grinned down at the comely Indian maiden who had cast her lot with the white settlers as a means of helping her tribesmen to a better destiny in the long run.

'General Grant and the white settlers of Oregon and California will never forget yore part in tonight's victory, Winema and Frank,' Captain Bob Pryor said. 'I'm shore of that.'

He did not know it, but the Rio Kid spoke more truly than he knew. A grateful Oregon legislature was to vote a life-long pension to Winema, the 'Oregon Pocahontas,' and her loyal husband.

Major Tracy Williard, bleeding from a superficial arm wound, walked over to where the Rio Kid and Celestino stood side by side. The Army commander, instead of being flushed with victory, shook his head sadly as he stared at the corpse of Miles Elkorn.

'He had my complete trust and confidence,' said the disillusioned officer. 'Without his smuggled supplies, Captain Jack would have been forced to surrender months ago. So much expenditure of blood and treasure could have been averted if traitors such as Miles Elkorn were never born.'

Williard shook himself out of his mood and gestured toward Captain Jack and his captive chieftains.

'A circuit court in Jackson County has

136

indicted those Modoc chiefs to stand trial for killing white settlers,' he said. 'They will pay for their crimes on the gallows.'

* * *

Four months later, in October, Williard's prediction was to come true when Captain Jack and his lieutenants, the scourge of the Oregon country, met their doom at rope's end.

'Words are futile things at a time like this, Captain Pryor,' Williard said. 'General— President Grant knew what he was doing when he assigned you to my command. History books of the future will give you the lion's share of the credit for ending the Modoc War, I am certain of that.'

The Rio Kid shook his head.

'Thank yuh, Major,' he said. 'But Celestino and I do our work under cover so far as the Army is concerned. As a matter of fact, we already have orders to report to Fort Laramie up in Wyomin' as soon as this job is finished, to carry out another assignment. I only hope we'll be as fortunate in our new commandin' officer as we have been with you, Major Williard, in trappin' the Lion of the Lavabeds.'

We hope you have enjoyed this Large Print book. Other Chivers Press or Thorndike Press Large Print books are available at your library or directly from the publishers.

For more information about current and forthcoming titles, please call or write, without obligation, to:

Chivers Large Print
published by BBC Audiobooks Ltd
St James House, The Square
Lower Bristol Road
Bath BA2 3BH
UK
email: bbcaudiobooks@bbc.co.uk
www.bbcaudiobooks.co.uk

OR

Thorndike Press
295 Kennedy Memorial Drive
Waterville
Maine 04901
USA
www.gale.com/thorndike
www.gale.com/wheeler

All our Large Print titles are designed for easy reading, and all our books are made to last.